"*A tough man like you doesn't ever need or want a woman,*"

Jacqui taunted.

Spencer gave her a stunned look. "You don't know anything about me."

"I know what I see!" she flung at him.

She was breathing rapidly, her breasts heaving. His eyes ran up and down the length of her as if he needed evidence that she was a woman—a desirable woman.

"Do you? I doubt it."

"I see that you don't know anything about treating a woman right!"

His brown eyes blazed down at her and she braced herself, daring him to deny her accusation.

But his denial didn't come in the form of words. Suddenly he hauled her into his arms, and before she realized his full intention, his lips were on hers.

Dear Reader:

Happy holidays! Our authors join me in wishing you all the best for a joyful, loving holiday season with your family and friends. And while celebrating the new year—and the new decade!—I hope you'll think of Silhouette Books.

1990 promises to be especially happy here. This year marks our tenth anniversary, and we're planning a celebration! To symbolize the timelessness of love, as well as the modern gift of the tenth anniversary, each month in 1990, we're presenting readers with a *Diamond Jubilee* Silhouette Romance title, penned by one of your all-time favorite Silhouette Romance authors.

In January, under the Silhouette Romance line's *Diamond Jubilee* emblem, look for Diana Palmer's next book in her bestselling LONG, TALL TEXANS series—*Ethan*. He's a hero sure to lasso your heart! And just in time for Valentine's Day, Brittany Young has written *The Ambassador's Daughter*. Spend the most romantic month of the year in France, the setting for this magical classic. Victoria Glenn, Annette Broadrick, Peggy Webb, Dixie Browning, Phyllis Halldorson—to name just a few!—have written *Diamond Jubilee* titles especially for you. And Pepper Adams has penned a trilogy about three very rugged heroes—and their lovely heroines!—set on the plains of Oklahoma. Look for the first book this summer.

The *Diamond Jubilee* celebration is Silhouette Romance's way of saying thanks to you, our readers. We've been together for ten years now, and with the support you've given us, you can look forward to many more years of heartwarming, poignant love stories.

I hope you'll enjoy this book and all of the stories to come. Come home to romance—Silhouette Romance—for always!

Sincerely,

Tara Hughes Gavin
Senior Editor

STELLA BAGWELL

No Horsing Around

Silhouette *Romance*

Published by Silhouette Books New York

America's Publisher of Contemporary Romance

To Mr. Moon Thriller,
a magnificent racehorse

SILHOUETTE BOOKS
300 E. 42nd St., New York, N.Y. 10017

Copyright © 1990 by Stella Bagwell

ISBN: 0-373-08699-7

First Silhouette Books printing January 1990

Printed in the U.S.A.

Books by Stella Bagwell

Silhouette Romance

Golden Glory #469
Moonlight Bandit #485
A Mist on the Mountain #510
Madeline's Song #543
The Outsider #560
The New Kid in Town #587
Cactus Rose #621
Hillbilly Heart #634
Teach Me #657
The White Night #674
No Horsing Around #699

STELLA BAGWELL

is a small-town girl and an incurable romantic—a combination she feels enchances her writing. When she isn't at her typewriter, she enjoys reading, listening to music, sketching pencil drawings and sewing her own clothes. Most of all she enjoys exploring the outdoors with her husband and young son.

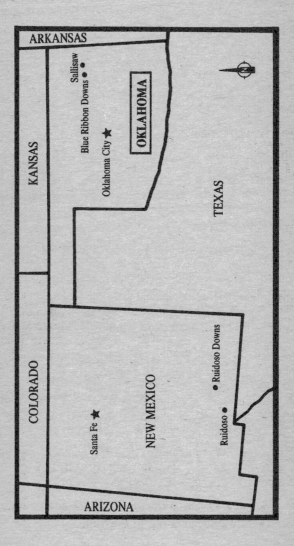

Prologue

Jacqueline Prescott was roused from her light slumber by the soft swish of the door being opened and closed.

She blinked her red, bleary eyes to see a white-coated doctor leaning over her uncle's hospital bed. Terror seized her heart as she realized she'd been asleep. Claude could have called out to her and she might not have heard. Even worse he could have . . .

Jacqui couldn't bear to think of her dear uncle's life coming to an end, even though she knew the end was near.

Taking a bracing breath, she rose to her feet just as the doctor pulled the stethoscope from his ears.

"How is he, Dr. Beattie?"

The tall gray-haired doctor shook his head grimly, then gently guided her out of the room.

Once they were in the corridor, he answered, "Not good, Jacqueline. His heartbeat is very irregular now. I expect fluid to start filling his lungs any day. It's only a matter of time."

Pain and sadness gripped Jacqui. "Please don't let him suffer," she whispered.

Dr. Beattie patted her slender shoulder in a comforting gesture. "I promise to do all I can. But right now I suggest you go home and rest. You'll be no help to Claude if you become ill, too."

"I will—later," she promised. "I just want to stay with him a little longer."

After the doctor left to continue his rounds, Jacqui went to stand beside her uncle's bed.

He was seventy-two, but his cancer-ridden body looked much older. He was as fragile as an autumn leaf. Jacqui knew it wouldn't be long until the winter wind of time carried him away from her. It was inevitable now.

She said a quick prayer, then walked over to the window that looked out over the hospital parking lot. Snow covered the ground and was heaped in piles between the parked cars. She figured the skiers had made a big day of it on Sierra Blanca.

Sighing wistfully as she watched the falling snow, she tried not to imagine what life would be like without Uncle Claude. She loved him just as any daughter could love a father. In fact, Claude had been her father for the past twelve years since a plane crash killed her parents.

Her father had been one of three sons, Claude being the oldest. She'd gone to live with him, mainly because they'd lived close to him and she'd known him better than any of her other relatives.

His wife had died years before and because they'd had no children, Claude had doted on Jacqui. Yet he'd raised her with a firm hand and a strong sense of morals.

She owed him so much. She loved him so much. Oh, Uncle Claude, her heart cried. Why do you have to leave me?

Jacqui went back to her chair beside the bed to keep her silent vigil. Eventually she must have slept because she woke again to the whispery sound of her uncle's voice.

Her heart pounding with dread, she leaned over his bed and grasped his thin, bony hand.

"I'm here, Uncle Claude," she assured him in a soft voice.

He opened his eyes and tried his best to smile at his niece. "You look tired Jacqui-Jane. You should go home."

Jacqui shook her head, the lump in her throat thickening at the nickname he always used for her. "I'm fine. I'll have a rest once your brother gets here."

"Hadley shouldn't be wasting time coming out here to see me," Claude said.

Jacqui's smile was tinged with sadness. "Hadley loves you."

"Hell girl, I know that," he said with a force that winded his frail body. "But there isn't a thing he can do here. I'll be leaving soon and nothing you or Hadley has to say about it will make a difference."

"Don't talk that way!"

Claude's white eyebrows pulled together in a frown. "Be sensible, Jacqui-Jane. We both know it's coming. That's why I need to know you'll be taken care of."

Jacqui soothed her fingers across the back of his hand. "I'm twenty-three now, Uncle. You know that I can take care of myself."

Claude's head moved faintly back and forth. "I don't give a damn how old you are! I've already spoken to Hadley about things. He wants you to come live with him."

"But why? My home is here in Ruidoso," she reasoned.

"Everyone needs to be near family. Even Hadley. Even you, Jacqui-Jane," Claude said wearily.

Jacqui let out a deep sigh. She didn't want to argue with her uncle, not at a time like this. But this couldn't be.

"Uncle, I'm getting good mounts now. The other jockeys and trainers respect my ability to ride. I can't give up horse racing. Not even for you. And you know that!"

A faint smile touched his mouth. "Foolish girl, I'm not asking you to give up racing. I didn't teach you all about horses for nothing. Hadley lives on a horse ranch, you know. Breeds good racing stock. Derby and futurity contenders. You'll like it there."

"Hadley has a partner, and from what I hear he deals with everything pertaining to the horses. Hadley only sees to the business side of things. How do you know this partner will welcome me just because I'm Hadley's niece?"

"Well, hell," Claude huffed impatiently. "Hadley's house is on the ranch. I don't guess this man can tell Hadley who can live in his own home!"

"But I want to ride!" Jacqui went on to the next foreseeable problem.

"Jacqui-Jane," he said fondly, sighing. "You will ride, darlin'. Blue Ribbon Downs isn't but a few miles away. It's a tough track, but I know you can compete with the best of them. There'll be plenty of trainers there needing a good jockey like you."

Jacqui didn't want to go to Oklahoma! New Mexico was her home. Her friends were here. Her career as a jockey was here at Ruidoso Downs, one of the most famous Thoroughbred and quarter horse racetracks in the southwest.

She wanted to tell her uncle this, but she loved him too much to upset him in any way. Now was not the time to go against his wishes. And from Claude's quickly deteriorating condition, she doubted there would be a right time for it in the future.

"You may be right, Uncle. I'll talk with Hadley about it when he gets here," she said in an effort to comfort him. "Now go back to sleep. I'll be here beside you."

He squeezed her hand and closed her eyes. Jacqui brushed his thin gray hair off his forehead and leaned down to kiss his cheek.

Tears scalded her eyes, but she did not allow them to fall. Claude didn't want her tears. He liked her strong and spunky. She was determined to give him that much. It was the only thing she could give him now.

Chapter One

Prescott Farms was located some ten miles from town. Hadley's instructions made it easy for Jacqui to find the place. It was nestled on flat bottom land with a few rolling hills near the ranch house itself.

Jacqui had made the eight hundred mile or so drive from Ruidoso in two and a half days. She was exhausted both mentally and physically, and it was a relief when she pulled over the cattle guard that led into the ranch's entrance.

The landscape was very different from the mountains of Ruidoso. Jacqui noted that even though it was only February, the hardwood trees had started to bud, and out in the pastures, green rye grass lay like a thick green carpet.

A white board fence ran for at least a mile on either side of the tree-lined lane. As Jacqui neared the house, she noticed yellow daffodils nodding their heads in the late afternoon sun, and a faint wisp of smoke trailed up from the rock chimney.

Jacqui parked the car in the driveway. She climbed out slowly, flexing her arms and legs to ease their stiffness from the long drive.

There was a cool wind from the north, but Jacqui found it pleasant after being cooped up in her small car. The breeze whipped her long auburn hair and she reached up to catch it as she took a moment to study the big rock house.

It was an L-shaped structure with a wide concrete porch running along the front. To the left of it was a gazebo made of pretty white latticework. Some fifty yards east of the house was a big red barn, then next to it, several more low-shedded barns that were obviously horse stables.

Everything looked well maintained, the house and grounds were lovely and she knew her Uncle Hadley welcomed her. But Jacqui was suddenly filled with fresh sadness. Seeing this place that was to be her new home reminded her all over again that her beloved Claude was gone. She missed him so. She missed Ruidoso. Could Prescott Farms ever take its place? she wondered dismally.

A faint noise had Jacqui's head turning back to the house. She smiled as she saw Hadley walking out to greet her.

"I see you made it safely," he said with a wide grin.

Hadley was a tall, muscular man with reddish-brown hair that was grizzled with gray. At the moment it was covered with a blue cap that said Prescott Farms on the front.

"Yes," she said. "How are you, Uncle Hadley?"

"I'm glad you've come, Jacqui. Claude wanted you here and so do I." He curved his arm around her shoulder and hugged her affectionately.

Jacqui looked up at him and summoned a smile. She hadn't seen him since Claude's funeral. At that time she'd been so grief stricken over Claude's death that she didn't think she would have made it without Hadley's comforting presence.

"You're a kind man, Uncle Hadley," she told him.

Hadley rubbed the top of her head in a gesture of fondness. "I didn't realize you were so short. You're a tiny little thing. Just like your mother was, I remember."

"Thank you for having me," Jacqui told him. His warm affection was soothing. She'd felt so cold and empty since Claude's passing. Maybe being near Hadley was going to lessen her loss. Right now she'd be thankful for anything to relieve the ache in her heart.

Hadley patted her shoulder then turned to her car. "Don't start thanking me now," he said teasingly. "After I put you to work around here, you may not feel so good about your old Uncle Hadley."

He pulled her bags out of the trunk, and Jacqui moved to help him. After a couple of trips, they had all her cases deposited in a bedroom at the far end of the house.

A print spread of apricot and apple green covered the four-poster. Curtains of the same fabric were pulled back from the wide-paned window, giving Jacqui a view of one of the pastures. She took a moment to see that it was dotted with huge elm and oak trees.

Beneath the bare limbs, four yearlings grazed and frolicked. Jacqui's heart lifted as she watched them.

Horses were her life and she loved them passionately. Claude had been in the racing business long before she had gone to live with him. Down through the years he'd produced many winners, and he'd taught Jacqui all about the business. It was comforting in a way that Hadley was just as fond of racing as Claude had been.

Hadley left Jacqui to go tell the housekeeper to prepare them a pot of fresh coffee. Jacqui busied herself with unpacking a few of her cases.

Several minutes later she was sitting on a long couch in the living room, sipping hot coffee. Hadley was in a big leather recliner positioned near the fireplace, his muddy boots crossed at the ankles.

"Will you have cold weather for much longer?" she asked.

He shook his head. "By mid-March it begins to warm up. By May it will be so hot, you'll be wanting to go back to Ruidoso," he told her.

Jacqui looked into the brown liquid in her cup. "There's not much there for me now," she said, barely aware of just how dispirited she sounded.

Hadley's blue eyes squinted, then filled with concern as he studied his niece. "I know it was hard to see your and Claude's home sold to strangers. I know he was like your father. I can't take his place, but I'll always be here for you."

She looked up at Hadley. Tears blurred her vision as she tried to smile at him. He was opening up his heart to her, and she suspected that in a way Hadley needed her as much as she needed him now that Claude had been taken from them.

Placing her china cup on a low table in front of her, Jacqui rose to her feet and crossed the room to her uncle.

"At first I told Claude I didn't want to come here," she admitted, taking a seat on the arm of his chair. "I was afraid of being an outsider. But I'm getting the feeling that you're not going to let that happen. Thank you, Uncle Hadley," she said huskily and leaned over and kissed his cheek.

He patted her arm and beamed a smile at her. "You know, Jacqui, after Emma and I divorced, I never remarried, so I don't have a family of my own. The only thing close to it was Claude, and we didn't get to see each other as much as we should have. I regret that now. It's gonna be nice having you around. And if I make too much of a fuss over you, just remember I never had a little girl to spoil."

She laughed softly, feeling her heart lift. "I'll remember."

"Am I interrupting?"

Startled by a third voice, Jacqui turned her head toward the doorway. In it stood a tall, lean man. A black Stetson was pulled low over his forehead, and a black denim shirt covered his broad chest.

He was an imposing figure, Jacqui thought. She was even more certain of it when his dark eyes cut her an inquisitive look.

"Not at all, Spencer," Hadley told the younger man. "I'm glad you dropped by. Jacqui arrived just a few minutes ago."

Spencer stepped farther into the room. So this was Hadley's niece, he thought, doing his best to hide his surprise. She was nothing like he'd been expecting.

"Jacqui, this is Spencer Matlock, my partner and the trainer here at Prescott Farms," Hadley informed her.

Jacqui rose gracefully and crossed the room to the other man.

"It's very nice to meet you, Mr. Matlock," she said, holding her hand out to him. "Uncle Hadley speaks very highly of you."

The strong hand that took hold of Jacqui's tiny one was large, warm and work-callused. She was struck both by his touch and the wry twist to his mouth.

"There's times Hadley can't stand me. But he likes the way I handle the horses and the ranch."

"I'm certain he does," Jacqui murmured as he released her.

She turned to take a seat on the couch. Spencer's dark brown eyes followed her movements. Hadley had told him she'd been jockeying out at Ruidoso Downs. That fact amazed him now. Not because she was a woman, but because of the kind of woman she was.

Spencer was sure she couldn't have been much over five foot two and she couldn't have weighed more than a hundred and five pounds. Since she was jockeying, he'd expected her to be small, but he hadn't expected her to have curves in all the right places.

She was wearing black tailored slacks with a white silk blouse. A paisley scarf of copper and gold colors was tied loosely around her neck. The colors picked up the fiery glints in her auburn hair.

This woman was soft, feminine, graceful, with a voice to match. And she was beautiful. Spencer hated to admit it, but how could he not, when the fact was staring him in the face.

"I was just telling Jacqui how glad I was to have her here. She's going to make this place seem more like a home now."

Spencer looked at Hadley and noticed the joy on the older man's face. It was obvious he was already attached to his niece. He was glad for Hadley. His brother Claude had been the only family he had as far as Spencer knew. But as far as Spencer was concerned, he wasn't glad that Jacqueline Prescott had come here to make her home. She meant trouble. He could feel it in his bones.

Gertrude had let it slip to him that a few years ago Jacqui had divorced her husband less than a year after they'd married. The man had apparently been a struggling horse trainer, just as Spencer had once been. In his opinion, Jacqui was no better than his mother or late wife had been. Neither one of them had possessed enough love and respect to stand beside their husbands. It was obvious to Spencer that Jacqui hadn't, either.

Spencer turned back to the auburn-haired woman. "Hadley tells me you're from Ruidoso," he said.

She nodded. "Yes, I've lived there since I was very small." She motioned toward the insulated pot the housekeeper had left behind. "Would you like coffee, Mr. Matlock?"

"Yes. Thank you."

She poured him a cup and he reached to take it from her. She noticed he ignored the cream and sugar sitting on the low table.

Spencer went to stand by the hearth some few feet away from Hadley, and Jacqui took note of the casual grace of his body as he moved across the room.

There was a pair of leather gloves jammed in his back pocket and mud stained his cowboy boots. She guessed he'd been at work since before daybreak. From living with Claude, she knew a horse trainer's job was never ending.

Hadley had told her that Spencer had been married, but his wife had died in an automobile accident some eight years ago. He was a very attractive man in a rough, masculine way. She wondered if he'd ever been tempted to marry again.

"Hadley says you've been jockeying at Ruidoso Downs. Quarter horses or Thoroughbreds?"

She warmed to his question and her oval face lit from within as she smiled. "Both."

His eyes narrowed just a fraction. "And which do you prefer?"

"I love both kinds of horses," she admitted. "But that quick burst of speed on a quarter horse is really exhilarating."

Jacqui thought she saw him frown as he lifted the coffee cup to his lips.

Hadley spoke up. "You should be happy here then, Jacqui, because Spencer deals in both kinds of horses."

Her smile moved to Hadley. "Before Claude died he often talked of the horses you had here on Prescott Farms. I can't wait to see them," she said.

Hadley drained the last of his coffee, then pushed himself out of the recliner. "And you shouldn't have to wait. Why don't you go change? Spencer and I will show you around."

"I'll be right back," she eagerly promised and hurried down to her room.

When she returned a few moments later wearing a pair of faded jeans, boots and thick white sweater, Hadley was gone from the room. Jacqui looked questioningly at Spencer.

"Where did Uncle Hadley get off to?"

Not bothering to look at her, Spencer set his coffee cup down on the table in front of the couch.

"He had a long-distance phone call from Bossier City. He said for us to go on without him. He'll catch up later."

"Oh. Well, my look around can wait. I'm sure you're busy," she said. She had the distinct feeling that Spencer didn't like her for some reason. She didn't know why, especially since he didn't know her. Still, there was something about the way he looked at her that made her feel cold and hot at the same time.

He shrugged. "I have to go down to the stables anyway. Come if you like."

Jacqui smiled at him even though his stern features didn't invite it. "I'll come then," she said.

Outside Spencer set a brisk pace toward the stables. Jacqui's shorter legs moved quickly to keep up with him. As they walked in silence she studied her surroundings. They were all so new and strange. There weren't any snowcapped mountains hovering above, no dense pines or tall thick fir trees. She could already feel that the air was much heavier than in Ruidoso, which had an elevation of over seven thousand feet. Jacqui figured Sallisaw was going to be humid and sultry by the time the warm spring weather arrived.

Pushing her hand through her slightly wavy hair, Jacqui looked over at Spencer Matlock. It was going to take a while for her to become acclimatized to more than just the weather around here, she thought.

They reached a board fence and she waited while Spencer opened the gate. She stepped through it ahead of him, her eyes on three horse walkers some yards away from the stables. Presently five horses were hooked to one of the machines and being walked in a circle.

"Claude raised horses, too, didn't he?"

Spencer's voice had Jacqui turning her attention from the horses back to him. She nodded. "Yes. But these last few years he had to sell out because of his failing health."

There was a haunted, sad look in her green eyes when she spoke of Claude. Spencer didn't want to acknowledge it, however. He didn't want to think of her as someone who loved and cared for others. She was a rebel just like Danielle had been. Jacqui's divorcing her husband proved it, and he wanted nothing to do with her.

"So you took to riding," he mused aloud, his voice a bit sardonic. "I don't suppose you ever made the All American Futurity?"

The question wasn't meant to be a question. It was meant as an insult. The All American Futurity, which was held at Ruidoso Downs each year, was one of the biggest quarter horse races in the United States, the purse paying over a hefty two million dollars. Jacqui supposed Spencer believed the closest she'd ever gotten to a race of that caliber was watching it from the grandstands.

She didn't understand this man, or why he'd chosen to be antagonistic toward her. Normally it wouldn't bother her that much, but grief over Claude's death had left her raw and vulnerable. She needed a friend now more than ever. It was too bad that Spencer had already decided he didn't want to be her friend.

"I rode a colt in the trial heats," she told him without any smugness. "I was beat out of the Futurity only by two hundredths of a second. I was disappointed, but Uncle Claude was very proud about the whole thing anyway."

He didn't seem to believe her, and Jacqui felt herself grow hot as he studied her face, then gazed down to the slim line of her throat and her small breasts beneath the white sweater.

He finally lifted his eyes back to her face, but the look he gave her was masked. "I had a colt in training that I hoped would be a contender. But he shinbucked a month before the trial heats."

Jacqui felt sick at his clipped words. Shin-bucking was an ugly thing. Sometimes when a young horse was giving it his all-out best, the strain on his front legs would become too great, causing the flesh to pull away from the bone. The injury took months to heal and Jacqui hated to see it happen to any horse.

"I'm sorry about that, Mr. Matlock. Perhaps this year you'll do better. I hope the colt is healed now."

Spencer was taken aback by her sincere words and genuine concern for the horse—especially after the remark he'd made to her about riding in the All American. He didn't know what had made him say it. Whatever the reason, he regretted it now. The mocking quality disappeared from his voice.

"He's coming along very well. Would you like to see him?"

Jacqui was surprised by his question and she decided Spencer Matlock was like a chameleon. She wondered what color he was going to show her next.

The horse was at the end of the long shed row. He was sorrel with a tiny white star on his forehead.

Spencer opened the stall and slipped a halter over the horse's head. Jacqui stood back when he led the horse out, but moved in for a closer inspection once he was in the open.

"He's gorgeous," she said.

Spencer noticed the glow on Jacqui's face as she smoothed a hand over the horse's sleek shoulder. It had been a long time since he'd seen a woman so vibrant or beautiful. Her eyes were huge and green with a faint slant to them, and her skin was soft and milky white.

"Have you run him since he's healed?"

Spencer nodded. "At four hundred and forty yards. He won it."

Jacqueline smiled and her eyes sparkled with excitement, as if the race had just taken place. "That's a tough distance. I'll bet Hadley was thrilled about the win."

He gave a short laugh. "Hadley loves to win."

And so did Spencer Matlock, she could already see he was that kind of man. Squatting down on her boot heels, Jacqui ran her hands softly over the horse's front legs. They seemed sound enough and she had to silently admit that Spencer must know his business.

Jacqui stood and patted the horse's neck. She could feel Spencer's eyes on her and she wondered what he was thinking. Even more, she wondered how she was going to work with this man. She had never been around a man who could make her think about him instead of the horse. But Spencer Matlock did, and she wasn't quite sure why.

Then she quickly reminded herself that she'd had one disastrous relationship with a horse trainer. She wasn't about to jump into the frying pan to be burned by another one.

"How many horses do you have here at Prescott Farms?" she asked, meeting his sharp brown eyes.

He rubbed a hand across his square jaw. Jacqui had already noticed his hair was sandy colored, which should have made his complexion fair, but instead he was rather dark. Jacqui supposed his coloring came from working outside the year around.

"Twenty-five currently in training. Eleven of those are owned by the farm, the others are owned by outside interests. The farm also has ten brood mares, all of which are due to foal by April. Three of them are due any day."

"Where are they kept?" she asked.

He nodded toward the big barn standing behind the stables. "That's the foaling barn. I'll show you," he said.

Jacqui nodded and waited while he put the young sorrel back in the stall. After he'd secured the bolt on the door they began to stroll through the length of the shed row.

The clean smell of wood shavings filled the air, along with the pungent odor of prairie hay. Jacqui noticed the stalls and the horses were spotlessly groomed.

"How many people work for you?" she questioned as they stepped from beneath the shade of the building.

"Three. One does the galloping and the other two handle the feeding, grooming and cleaning the stalls."

"I'd be happy to help with the galloping," she offered quickly.

His thin lips lifted at one corner. "I should have known you wouldn't offer to shovel manure."

Jacqui stiffened at his sardonic attitude. "That wasn't what I meant. I'd be happy to help clean stalls, too. I'm certainly not above that. It's just that I've been galloping for years now. Up until Uncle Claude died I worked down at the track galloping for different trainers from six to twelve, five days a week."

And working around all those men, he thought. He'd bet they swarmed around her like bees to honey. It was probably why she'd chosen to be in the business. Suddenly he felt unreasonably angry.

"I suppose you've talked to Hadley about helping with the horses."

The tone of his voice was strictly business, and Jacqui made certain hers matched it. "Yes, as a matter of fact, I have. He believes I'm capable of doing the job as well as the next man. And I will, if given the chance," she added.

They had continued to walk as they talked, but now Spencer suddenly stopped and turned to face her. She was keenly aware of a strange glitter in his dark eyes that spoke of smothered hostility.

"Look, Miss Prescott, I think it would be better if I made myself clear right from the start. You may know all about horses and maybe you're a damn good jockey, but just don't expect to come in here and take a free rein. Hadley only tends to the business end of things. I own and train the horses on the farm. The way I see fit," he added pointedly. "I'll accede to you galloping here on the farm. But as far as jockeying any of my races, you might as well forget it."

Jacqui stood looking up at him, completely stunned. She'd never had anyone, man or woman, treat her with such obvious disrespect. It was blatantly apparent that he deeply resented her. The realization hurt, not just because he doubted her ability to ride, but because he doubted her as a person. She had always had a natural fondness for all people, and she wanted them to like her in return. It looked as if that wasn't to be with Spencer Matlock.

She lifted her chin with a certain amount of pride. Claude had always wanted her to remember she was a lady, but he'd also wanted her to stand up for herself. She kept that in mind as she locked eyes with Spencer.

"Maybe I should make something clear, too, Mr. Matlock. I understand that I'm not known around here, and that I'll have to prove myself as a jockey all over again. I don't expect top contenders to be handed

to me. But I made a darn good living jockeying out at
Ruidoso, and I fully intend to do the same thing here
at Blue Ribbon Downs. With or without your horses,
or your blessing.''

His face paled at her words and Jacqui knew she'd
angered him. Yet that hardly mattered, she thought.
For some unknown reason, this man had decided not
to like her long before he'd ever met her.

"If it's all the same to you, I'll wait for my uncle to
finish the tour," she said, turning on her boot heel and
starting back toward the house.

"I'm friends with the biggest part of the owners and
trainers around here. I could make it hard for you."

The words slowed her steps but did not stop her. She
cast him a glance over her shoulder. He looked hard
and cold standing there by the barn, his long legs
planted apart, his arms crossed over his broad chest,
and Jacqui wondered what had made him that way. "I
really doubt it, Mr. Matlock. But go ahead and try if
that will make you happy.''

Jacqui didn't wait to see what kind of response, if
any, he would give her. She'd had enough of the man
for one day.

Chapter Two

Ho, where's the fire?" Hadley said with a booming voice and a low chuckle.

Jacqui had just rounded the corner of the stables and collided with her uncle's broad chest.

His hands shot out to steady her. Jacqui caught her breath before she looked up at him. "I—I was coming to find you."

He looked beyond her toward the foaling barn. "Where's Spence? Did he show you around?"

Jacqui's eyes drifted to the ground and the toes of her red boots. "Partly. I decided I'd rather wait for you."

Hadley studied the top of her head. "Is something wrong? Did you and Spence get crossways?"

She lifted her head and gave him a wry smile. "Not exactly crossways. Your trainer doesn't like me."

Hadley threw his head back and laughed, which made Jacqui even more confused.

"Spence doesn't have much to do with women. Don't take it personally." Grinning, he added, "I expected you to be a bee under his collar."

"Uncle Hadley! I don't want to stir up a hornet's nest around here. You should have warned me about him."

Still smiling, Hadley shook his head. "Don't worry about it. Spencer will get used to having you around."

Jacqui doubted that, but she didn't voice her thoughts. "He agreed to let me help with the galloping," she told him.

One of Hadley's thick brows lifted with wry speculation. "Well, that's a start."

Jacqui didn't want to ask what kind of start. "I'm sure he's an excellent trainer, or he wouldn't be here. But he's..." She couldn't finish. There just wasn't any way she could sum up the man. Not yet at least.

Hadley patted her shoulder and led her back toward the barns. "Spencer is a good, dedicated man. He just seems a bit cold if you don't know him. But he'll come around, Jacqui," he assured her. "Once he sees how good you are with horses, there won't be any problem."

Jacqui didn't know what to make of the whole thing. But she did know that Hadley had opened his home to her, and she didn't intend to stir up any sort of trouble. She figured the best thing to do would be to stay as far away from Spencer Matlock as she possibly could.

From what her uncle had told her earlier, there were many training stables in the area. She had a good record at Ruidoso, surely she could land mounts in a few races. As she'd told Spencer, she didn't need him.

"Don't worry, Uncle, I have no intention of causing trouble."

Hadley laughed. "Who's worried about trouble? So come along, darlin', and we'll look at Spencer's brood mares."

They caught up with Spencer in the foaling barn. Jacqui met his cool gaze, then avoided him completely as they looked at first one mare and then the other. Hadley and Spencer talked at some length about each one and the foals they were expecting soon. Jacqui listened quietly and eyed the beautiful horses around her.

Once they were back outside, Hadley steered Jacqui in the direction of another row of stables.

"The farm's Black Gold contender is over here, Jacqui. I want you to take a look at him. Spencer broke him a few months back. The jockey has been galloping him for some time now, and has worked him out of the gates a few times," Hadley told her.

Jacqui could easily pick up the pride on Hadley's face and in his voice as he reached for the halter hanging outside the stall door. He handed the halter to Spencer. "Get him out, Spence, and show Jacqui."

Spencer took the halter from Hadley and entered the stall. A moment later he came out leading a black colt.

"He was two this January, so his legs should be well developed by race time."

Jacqui looked at the young stallion with a shrewd eye. He was a beauty indeed, long-bodied and long-legged. She could see the Thoroughbred bloodlines mixed with that of the heavier quarter horse.

"He's certainly nice and long," Jacqui commented. "And I like the muscles on his hips and shoulders."

"You like them," Spencer mocked her modest compliment. "He has more muscle than some three-year-olds."

She took her eyes off the colt to look at Hadley's trainer. "I've come to learn that muscle isn't everything, Mr. Matlock." Even in men, she wanted to add. She took a deep breath and went on. "If a horse doesn't run with his heart, then all the muscle in the world won't help him."

"This one will have the heart," Hadley spoke up. "His mama and papa both ran triple A time. He has the desire to run bred in him."

"What's his name?" Jacqui asked.

"Bold Tyrant," Spencer answered.

Jacqui stepped forward and stroked the stallion's nose. He nudged her gently on the shoulder, but didn't bite as many stallions would have. Jacqui could see that Spencer had taught this one good manners. Bold Tyrant had the marking of a winner and just looking at the horse left Jacqui with a rush of excitement.

The Black Gold Futurity was run at Blue Ribbon Downs. Jacqui was not the only New Mexican familiar with the race. It had a six-figure purse and carried a prestigious honor. To win it on a horse such as this one was something Jacqui had always dreamed of.

She looked at Spencer once again. "You've certainly taught him good manners."

He arched a brow at Jacqui and his mouth hinted at a smile. "Most people think my horses are better mannered than I am. What do you think, Miss Prescott?"

His dry humor surprised her, and she thought once again what a complex man he was.

Knowing he was deliberately putting her on the spot in front of Hadley, she treated his question lightly. "I don't really know you, Mr. Matlock. Ask me again in a few days," she told him.

Something flared in his brown eyes as they looked at Jacqui's. She saw it and felt it. Then his hand reached up and slid slowly, tenderly, against the colt's neck and Jacqui felt something twist inside her. This man wasn't a rock. He just wanted to pretend that he was.

"I probably will," he said, then turned to lead Bold Tyrant back into the stall.

Hadley suddenly spoke up. "Gertrude is making a big meal for Jacqui tonight. Why don't you come over, Spencer? I'll have her add an extra plate."

Jacqui wanted to strangle her uncle and she silently held her breath as Spencer finished latching the stall. Maybe he would turn down the invitation, she hoped.

"Is six-thirty early enough?" he asked instead.

Hadley grinned. "Fine. We'll see you then," he said, and started back to the house.

Jacqui silently followed, trying her best to hide her uneasiness. She definitely wasn't looking forward to supper.

Hadley's housekeeper, Gertrude, was a pleasant woman in her late fifties. She was plump and plain-faced, and she had a warm smile and a happy attitude.

Jacqui liked her immediately and she spent the remaining part of the day in the kitchen with Gertrude.

"I've never been to New Mexico," she told Jacqui as she stirred a boiling mixture that would eventually become chocolate frosting for a cake.

"Then I'll have to take you sometime. It's very beautiful at Ruidoso. If we went in late summer, we could stop in the Hondo Valley and get fruit and honey. There's always chili peppers, too. Do you ever cook with peppers?"

Gertrude shook her head. "I don't know much about Mexican cooking, but I'd like to learn. It wouldn't hurt for Hadley to breathe a little fire once in a while," she said with a chuckle.

"I'd be glad to show you what I know," Jacqui put in.

Gertrude looked over her shoulder at Jacqui. "Hadley tells me you ride the horses. I didn't expect you to know how to cook."

Jacqui laughed softly. "Well, I do know about womanly things, too. I just don't have much time to do them."

"You gonna be riding for Spencer?" Gertrude asked.

Jacqui's brows pulled together. Spencer Matlock's threatening words were still very much with her. "I would like to, Gertrude. Spencer has some fine horses. But I guess we'll just have to wait and see."

Gertrude continued to stir her chocolate confection. "Spencer is a nice man," she told Jacqui in a thoughtful voice. "But he can be a moody one, too. I have a soft spot for him, though. He's had so much heartache in the past. Land sakes, if I'd went through with Jack what Spencer did with his wife..." She let out a deep sigh. "Well, I just don't think I could've made it. Course my husband passed on a couple years back. But Mrs. Matlock—Danielle—well she... It was just real tragic. I don't think Spencer has ever gotten over it."

Jacqui stared thoughtfully at Gertrude's back. What was the older woman saying? She opened her mouth to ask, then promptly shut it. Spencer Matlock's past or present was none of her business. She needed to remember that.

"It's a terrible hurt to lose someone you love," she finally remarked. And obviously Spencer had loved his wife dearly if he still wasn't able to overcome the trauma of losing her.

Gertrude glanced over her shoulder. "I don't know about love, miss, but I do know that Spencer changed after that wife of his died."

Jacqui reached for a tomato and quickly sliced it into wedges, mulling over Gertrude's words. Was the older woman trying to tell her that all had not been well in Spencer Matlock's marriage? Jacqui wasn't about to ask. She'd just remember to tread lightly whenever he was around.

Jacqui decided at the last minute to change out of her boots and jeans for supper. Hadley wasn't formal and if it had only been she and her uncle for supper, she wouldn't have bothered, but she didn't want to appear disrespectful to Spencer.

She chose a soft pink sweater and skirt that clung to her tiny curves. Although she was a redhead, her hair was dark enough and her complexion neutral enough to get away with wearing pink and other colors that some redheads had to avoid.

After brushing out her thick hair, she tied it back from her face with a wide pink ribbon, allowing it to fall down to her back in loose waves. She applied a dash of pink lipstick and blush, then deciding she'd paid enough attention to her appearance, left the bedroom to find her uncle.

Hadley was in the living room and much to her surprise, Spencer was already there with him. Both men turned as she entered. She smiled at her uncle, then nodded briefly at Spencer.

"I was just pouring us a glass of wine. Care to join us, Jacqui?" Hadley asked.

"I'd like that, thank you," she answered.

He poured a small measure into a goblet from a glass decanter, then handed the drink to her.

She carried it over by the fireplace and took a seat in an easy chair.

"What has Gertrude cooked tonight? Smells like roast beef," Hadley said.

"It is," Jacqui told him. "Along with several more dishes. She has enough food in there to feed three people for a week."

Hadley laughed. "You'll have to watch her, Jacqui, she'll try her best to fatten you up. She's already told me you're entirely too thin. She says you'd be just about like a mosquito up there on a horse's back."

"Once she sees how much I eat, she won't worry about me."

As if Gertrude knew they were discussing her, the older woman appeared in the doorway.

"Hadley, there's a man waiting to see you down by the stables."

He looked at his housekeeper. "Who is it?" he asked with faint annoyance.

She grinned broadly. "It's the man with the paint colt you wanted. I believe he wants to sell now," she said, obviously happy to be the bearer of good news.

Hadley glanced back at Jacqui and Spencer. "You two relax with your wine while I go try to make a horse deal. Hopefully this won't take long."

Jacqui watched him go with sinking dread. She wasn't looking forward to being alone with Spencer.

"I didn't know Hadley had any interest in buying horses for himself," she commented.

Spencer carried his wineglass over to the hearth, where he turned his back to the warmth of the fire. "He usually doesn't. But paint racing is still in its infancy. Hadley likes to think of himself as a pioneer."

Jacqui's gaze slid up his tall frame and she gripped the goblet a bit tighter. Spencer wasn't wearing his Stetson and she could now easily see his face. With his looks in plain view, she realized he was even more striking than she'd first believed. She thought he was like a lean, tawny tiger. Beautiful enough to want to touch, but far too dangerous to try.

"So did Claude. I've noticed they're alike in a lot of ways," Jacqui replied.

Spencer didn't comment and silence stretched between them.

Finally Jacqui spoke again. "I'm hungry. Are you?"

It was such a simple, yet personal question that for a moment Spencer merely stared at her. She looked so dainty, so fragile and feminine. The soft, clean scent of her reminded him of spring rains and a pasture full of wildflowers.

"Yes, I am," he said, forcing his eyes to pull away from her. The room was suddenly small. Too small.

She sipped more of her wine, then asked, "Have you known Hadley a long time?"

He nodded. "Since I was a small boy. He and my father were good friends. Dad raised horses, too. But he's dead now."

His voice was emotionless, making it impossible for Jacqui to guess how long he'd been without his father.

"That's too bad. Is your mother still living?"

He turned and looked at Jacqui. She winced inwardly at the mocking twist to his features. "Yes. But I have no idea where she lives."

Jacqui was shocked by his cool, detached words. She really didn't know what to say. She felt as if anything would be the wrong thing.

Spencer seemed to know this. He went on to explain. "She divorced Dad when I was very young. She wasn't too interested in being a mother then, and she isn't now." His dark eyes settled point-blank on Jacqui's face. "You see, Dad was a struggling trainer back then, and my mother hated the life. She wanted much more than my father could give her."

Jacqui thought there was faint accusation in his voice. Accusation that was directed at her. It didn't make sense. Maybe he'd heard that she'd divorced a horse trainer, also. But even if he had, that was no reason to label her bad. Jay had been a rake of the worst kind. She'd been left with no other choice than divorce.

"My mother was killed when I was eight years old. That was a long time ago, but I still miss her. She was a kind, gentle person."

He looked at her, then turned away. "Hadley says your father was killed at the same time."

Jacqui nodded. "Yes. They were racing people, also. They'd flown up to Albuquerque to watch the horses run at the fair. On the way back, their little plane ran into a blizzard. They went down in the mountains."

Feeling suddenly restless, she rose from the chair and walked over to the picture window that looked out over the portion of yard where the gazebo sat.

"I wonder how much longer Hadley will be?" she asked, looking over her shoulder at him. The fire glowed behind him, outlining his tall body. Even though he was lean, his shoulders were broad. Jacqui thought they looked very strong beneath the maroon-colored shirt he was wearing.

Her eyes meandered to his square jaw and thin lips, then farther up to his dark, piercing eyes. They were a sharp contrast to his sandy-colored hair, which waved subtly about his head. She suddenly wondered how old he was, and then she wondered why it should matter, and why she was looking at him in the first place.

Since her brief, disastrous marriage, men hadn't been a part of her life. Being a jockey was her prime ambition. Besides, Spencer Matlock was a man who would never invite her attentions anyway.

Spencer looked at Jacqui and felt his eyes drawn down the length of her. Beneath the miniskirt she was wearing, her legs looked incredibly smooth and gracefully curved. And suddenly he was wondering what it would be like to have her in bed with him, her white skin next to his, her long red hair cascading over the pillow.

He silently cursed himself for the thought and swallowed a large portion of wine. No woman had been in his bed since Danielle and he fully intended to keep it that way. Jacqueline Prescott was very young, too young for him. She reminded him of a spirited filly just learning to run, and he knew from past experience that once you let them have a free rein, they were never the same. Her poor ex-husband had obviously learned that the hard way.

"I say, I wonder how much longer it will be before Hadley returns?" she repeated, wondering at the odd look he was giving her.

He seemed to really see her then, and he shrugged at her words. "Hard to say. Would you like more wine?" he asked, crossing to a small bar in the corner of the room.

Jacqui watched him refill his glass. "No, thank you. I'm not used to alcohol, so this is more than enough," she told him.

Spencer took a seat at the end of the couch. Jacqui joined him on the opposite end, carefully cradling her glass in both hands. He looked down at her.

"It surprised me when Hadley told me you were coming here to live."

Jacqui was surprised that he was making conversation with her. She'd expected him to keep up his cold aloofness. Maybe this was a good sign.

"I was surprised myself," she admitted with a faint smile. "But it was what Uncle Claude wanted. I couldn't go against his wishes. He was very dear to me. Besides, it's nice being near family, and Uncle Hadley is about the only family I have left."

Without warning, Spencer was remembering Danielle. He could still hear her accusing him of being old-fashioned and stuffy because he hadn't wanted to move away from his father. Family had meant nothing to her. But then she hadn't wanted a family, not with Spencer.

Jacqui watched the hardening of his features and wondered what was running through his mind. Maybe he was doubting her reasons for coming here. Maybe he thought she was merely wanting a free meal ticket. That idea bothered her greatly.

"Eastern Oklahoma is very different from New Mexico," he said after a few moments. "But maybe you'll like it here."

"It's horse racing country," she told him, "and I like that about it."

"I suppose you left old friends behind," he continued.

Jacqui noticed his face was impassive as he spoke. She got the feeling he wasn't really interested in her answer, but merely making small talk.

"A few," she told him, glancing around at the warm, casual furnishings of the room. It bothered her to look at Spencer and she tried her best not to. But something about him kept pulling her eyes back. And each time she met his gaze, she felt herself growing warm and confused. "But I plan to go back for visits from time to time."

"Well," he drawled, leaning back against the couch and crossing his boots at the ankle. "I suppose you're one of those women who isn't interested in a long-term commitment with a man anyway."

Completely bewildered by his comment, Jacqui frowned. "I believe I'd want to be in love first. And no, I'm not one of those women. It's just that for the past few years I've been very dedicated to my career as a jockey. Besides, I'm only twenty-three."

"And you want to kick up your heels while you're still young," he added sardonically.

Jacqui was determined not to let him anger her. "Kick up my heels," she repeated with a soft laugh. "After riding horses all day, the only thing I look forward to is going to bed."

His brows lifted and Jacqui noted they were deep brown. His eyelashes were dark, too, except for the gold-tipped ends.

"Don't you find that boring?" he persisted.

Jacqui couldn't fathom the reason for his questions but she answered as best she could anyway.

"Why would it bore me? All day long I'm doing something I enjoy. Are you bored after training horses all day?"

"Touché, Ms. Prescott."

Jacqui flushed and dropped her eyes to the wineglass in her hands. "I wish you wouldn't call me Ms. Prescott," she told him. "It makes me feel dowdy."

Spencer amazed her with a grin. "Dowdy, eh? Well, Mr. Matlock makes me feel very old."

"Then do you think we could quit torturing each other with formality?" she asked.

He uncrossed his ankles and placed his empty glass on the coffee table. "Call me anything you like. I'm used to it," he told her blithely.

"Spencer will be fine. And as for me, Jacqui will do," she informed him with a slight grimace.

"Okay, Jacqui," he said after a moment. "But just don't think that getting on first-name basis will change my mind about you."

Jacqui's body stiffened on the couch. "What do you mean?" His face was blank, making it impossible for her to know what he was thinking.

"About my horses and your riding."

She suddenly felt very sad and hurt. She would truly like to be friends with Spencer, but she could see that he was never going to allow that. He'd already tried her for something, and the verdict was guilty. For what, she wasn't quite sure. Jacqui just hoped that once he got to know her, he would change his mind.

"No," she said carefully. "I won't forget. Now if you'll excuse me, I'm going to go check with Gertrude to see if she needs any help in the kitchen."

Spencer watched her leave the room. Her hair was like a dark flame caressing her back, and her body begged his eyes to follow her movements. Its lithe gracefulness reminded him of a ballerina and, sighing with a bit of regret, once again he felt the urgent need to keep a wedge between them.

Jacqui Prescott knew all about horses. It was obvious in the way she handled them, the way she rode them, and the way she loved and cared for them.

For weeks Spencer had kept a keen eye on Jacqui's movements. He'd been watching, almost hoping for her to make a wrong move or careless mistake with the horses. But she hadn't. In fact she had amazed him with her knowledge and ability.

At first Spencer had wanted to believe, for his own piece of mind, that she was a young woman merely playing at being a jockey. But he had to admit to himself that he could not fault her skill. Even more, she had been serious when she said she wasn't above cleaning stalls. More than once he'd walked through the shed row to find her helping the stable hands, David and Ken, two young men near Jacqui's age.

Neither one was married and Spencer could easily see from the very first day that both were smitten with her. She had a warm openness that invited a person to be her friend.

Except for Spencer. When he was around, she closed up like a morning glory. Spencer kept telling himself that was just the way he wanted it. After all, he didn't want to be close to Jacqui, he'd gone to extra lengths to let her know that from the moment they'd met.

Obviously it had worked. She didn't speak to him unless he asked her a direct question, and she certainly didn't smile at him as she did her uncle, David, Ken and J.T., the jockey who also galloped for Prescott Farms.

But Spencer was glad about that, too. He didn't want her smiles. He just wanted to forget she was even around.

Spencer checked the wrappings on a three-year-old, satisfying himself that the swelling in the Thorough-

bred's knees was going down, then left the stall. It was
the end of the day and the shadows were lengthening
across the barnyard. Spencer was tired and the thought
of going home to an empty house didn't help his frame
of mind.

A clear, tinkling laughter suddenly pulled him up
short. It was a woman's laugh.

Made curious by the unfamiliar sound, he skirted
around the back of the barn to investigate. There was
a small round pen connected to the barn that they used
for breaking yearlings. At the moment Jacqui and
Ken, a lanky blonde, were helping David, the smaller
dark-haired stable hand, up off the ground.

In one corner of the dusty lot a bay-colored ponying horse was saddled with a racing saddle and rolling
his eyes suspiciously at the three humans.

"What in hell is going on?" Spencer snapped out.

Jacqui was still laughing and Spencer realized it was
the first time he'd heard her really laugh since she'd
arrived at Prescott Farms. He should have been happy
that she was finally coming out of her grief over her
uncle's death. But instead it irked him to find her enjoying herself with David and Ken.

Undaunted by his stony features, Jacqui laughed
once more. "David thinks he wants to be a jockey. So
I saddled up Jack and was giving him a few riding lessons."

Spencer's jaw set even tighter. "So why are you
rubbing your shoulder, David?"

Before David could say anything, Jacqui came to his
defense. "It's nothing, Spencer. Jack merely broke
into a trot and David couldn't hang on."

The dark-headed young man smiled sheepishly and cautiously flexed his arm in a testing motion. "I'm fine, Spencer."

Spencer let out a frustrated breath, then took off his hat and slowly raked his fingers through his hair.

"What made you think you could ride Jack with a racing saddle, David?" he asked. Any other time he would have found the whole episode amusing. But not with Jacqui encouraging it.

Red-faced, David glanced at Jacqui, then back to his boss. "Jacqui does it so well, and she's been giving me pointers."

Spencer folded his arms across his chest while behind him Ken nervously cleared his throat.

"Boy, if you keep listening to Jacqui, she'll have you standing on your head before too long."

Fury shot through Jacqui but she said nothing. She wasn't about to make a scene with Spencer in front of the two men who were her friends and co-workers.

Ken spoke up in her defense, surprising Jacqui. "Jacqui's a good jockey. She's ridden in the All American Futurity trials."

Spencer's nostrils flared as he turned around to the blond young man. "Yes, I know."

"And she was beaten out only by two hundredths of a second," David tacked on proudly.

Spencer turned back, cynicism marking his face. "Yes, I know that, too."

Now he probably thought she'd been bragging to David and Ken, when actually it had been her Uncle Hadley who'd been telling them all about her riding, Jacqui mused.

David went on before Spencer had the chance to light into him about riding his ponying horse.

"Jacqui's going to race tomorrow over at Blue Ribbon. Are you going to let me and Ken off to go watch her?"

This was news to Spencer and he turned a narrowed eye on Jacqui. She was wearing old jeans and a yellow wool sweater that had seen better days. Her wavy hair had been gathered back into a French braid, but after the day's work, wisps had loosened and now curled around her face and throat. Her face was free of makeup and her hands, jeans and boots were dusty and dirty, but he had never seen a more beautiful woman.

She pulsed with color from her rich fiery hair to her dark green eyes and the sweep of pink across her cheeks and lips. Just looking at her fueled the desperation inside of him.

"You're racing tomorrow?"

Jacqui nodded. All the joy and merriment had left her face. Now a challenging look was in her eyes as she met his stare. "Yes, I am."

After a dreadful moment of silence he turned back to the two stable hands. "How do you think these stalls will get cleaned if you two are over at the racetrack watching Jacqui?"

Ken said, "Tomorrow is Saturday. You usually let us watch your horses run on Saturday, and Mr. Wallstreet is running tomorrow."

It was true, and it galled Spencer as he realized he was going to have to give in. "Go then," Spencer told them. "But you better make sure you have your work done."

"Yes, sir, we will," David happily promised.

"Now get Jack and put him up," Spencer ordered. "And make sure you brush him down good," he tacked on as the two young men rushed off to see after the horse.

Jacqui stood there, watching David and Ken. Angry fire was coursing through her.

"Who are you riding for?"

Spencer's sharp question jolted her and she turned around to see that he had moved closer and was now towering over her.

"Palmer Kirkland." If it was possible, Jacqui thought his face hardened even more.

"Palmer Kirkland is forty-five and divorced. It's no secret that he likes women," he said dryly.

Fury shook her body. "And that's hard for you to understand, isn't it, Spencer? A tough man like you doesn't ever need or want a woman. Do you?" she taunted angrily.

The look on Spencer's face said he didn't know whether he was stunned or mad.

"You don't know anything about me," he gritted.

"I know what I see!" she flung at him.

She was breathing rapidly, causing her small breasts to heave. Spencer's gaze ran up and down the length of her as if reminding him all over again that she was a woman—a desirable woman.

"Do you? I somehow doubt it."

There was a cutting edge to his low voice. Yet Jacqui refused to allow it to put her off. "I see you wouldn't know how to treat a woman even if someone gave you lessons!"

Spencer's brown eyes blazed down at her, and she braced herself in a rigid stance, daring him to deny her accusation.

But Spencer's denial didn't come in the form of words. Instead he reached out and hauled her into his arms.

Before Jacqui realized his full intentions, her head was wedged in the curve of his arm. Shocked at the contact of his body, she struggled, her left fist reaching up to push against his shoulder. Spencer didn't seem to notice her protest. His head inched downward until his lips were on hers.

Like a traitor, Jacqui's mind came to a screeching halt at the intimate touch. Her fist uncurled and flattened against his chest, her body sagged limply against his.

Spencer was acutely aware of her capitulation. The soft feel of her surrendering body pierced him with a new unwelcome feeling.

Jacqui felt the pressure of his mouth change suddenly. It was no longer out to teach her a lesson. It was a gentle, searching touch, a tempting graze of mouth against mouth, tongue against tongue, inviting her to kiss him in return.

It was impossible to remain indifferent to his kiss. And that was what it was, Jacqui realized. A fullfledged kiss. One that was spinning her round and round, coiling everything inside her tighter and tighter.

How could she want this man? she wondered frantically.

Before she could answer that question, Spencer had broken the kiss and stepped away.

Jacqui looked up at him, feeling both shock and arousal. He'd treated her with insolence, and she'd ended up kissing him as though she adored him. The whole thing was so confusing to Jacqui that anger was renewed and fresh tears swamped her eyes.

"So Spencer Matlock is human after all," she bit out hoarsely.

"Jacqui—"

Before he could say another word, she pushed past him and ran sobbing across the uneven ground of the barnyard.

Spencer started after her, but by then she was beyond the gate and out of reach.

The next instant scuffling footsteps sounded behind him. He turned to see Ken and David.

"Where was Jacqui going like that? What did you say to her?" Ken asked in an accusing voice.

"She didn't do anything wrong. I was the one who made her saddle Jack. You should be jumping on me, instead of her," David said.

Ken and David had worked for Spencer since the time they were young teenagers. It was hard for him to believe they'd put their jobs in jeopardy just to come to Jacqui's defense. Spencer had expected her to cause trouble. It hadn't taken long for his assumption to come true.

"Nothing happened to Jacqui," he growled, never before feeling as frustrated as he did at this moment.

Both young men stood there glowering, as though they didn't believe him.

Spencer muttered, "Hell, boys! It's past work hours. Go home!"

Neither one of them budged, making Spencer jerk off his hat and swat it against his leg. "I didn't get on to Jacqui about saddling Jack! She was angry at me because...because I kissed her."

The last words had Ken and David swapping stunned looks. Their expressions angered Spencer even more. It was obvious they considered him too old and hard to ever think about a woman, much less kiss one.

Spencer turned on his boot heel and stalked off, leaving the two stable hands staring after him.

Jacqui banged through the kitchen door. Angry strides propelled her down through the hallway, the living room, and past the study where her uncle was sitting at his desk.

"Hey girl, come back here. What's your hurry?" he called out.

She sniffed, wiped her eyes and turned back to the open doorway leading into the study. Before she could say anything, Hadley spotted the tears that she was sure had already turned her nose and eyes red.

He left his desk and crossed to the doorway where she stood. "What's the matter, honey? Have you fallen from one of those damn horses?"

Jacqui shook her head. "Nothing like that. It's...it's Spencer. I'd like to kill him!"

"Spencer?" he asked. "What has he done?"

Jacqui's fury suddenly blazed at the question. "He's acted like an almighty ass! That's what!"

Hadley laughed. In the short time that Jacqui had lived in Prescott Farms, she had come to realize that he was a man who saw the good in most everything. He probably felt it was better to see her in this worked-up state of mind than to watch her face filled with grief over Claude.

"Maybe you should go yell at him instead of me," he suggested.

"You're right, Uncle. You're exactly right," she said, feeling certain that a calculating gleam shone from her eyes.

Chapter Three

The house Spencer lived in was on Prescott Farms and situated a quarter mile from Hadley's. While Spencer had been married to Danielle, they'd lived in town and he'd driven out everyday to the ranch to work. After Danielle's death, Hadley had talked him into moving onto the ranch permanently.

The house was old, it being the original ranch house that had been built years ago when another family had used the place to run cattle. When Hadley purchased the ranch and renamed it Prescott Farms, he'd built the bigger, modern house. Later, when Spencer had gone into partnership with Hadley, they'd renovated the original house for Spencer.

As Spencer entered the old rock house, he reminded himself that Hadley had always wanted him close because he loved him like a son. With an odd feeling of sadness, Spencer pulled off his hat and laid it on top of a maple desk, then reached up to unsnap the pearl fasteners on his Western shirt.

Hadley was probably the only person who did truly love him. His father had, but he was dead. His mother would be a stranger now. And Danielle? In the beginning she'd acted as though she'd cared. But that had proven to be just that—an act.

Spencer sank down on the couch, leaned his head back and wondered why he was thinking such maudlin thoughts. Kissing a woman wasn't supposed to make a man soft. But it did. Soft in the head and soft in the heart.

Annoyed at himself, he stood and pulled off his shirt. He needed a hot shower, but the house was growing uncomfortably chilly.

Spencer quickly built up the dying fire in the fireplace, then stood a moment on the rock hearth to make sure the logs caught flame and burned.

Moments later he was walking down the hallway toward the bathroom, rubbing his tired eyes, when a banging knock sounded at the front door.

Frowning, Spencer went to answer it, wondering who it could be at this hour. It was practically dark and he and Hadley had already talked over the day's work. He didn't have time for casual friends, thus he never had much company.

"Spencer, I want to talk to you!"

Jacqui's voice blasted him as he opened the door and flipped on the porch light.

For a moment he merely stared at her, stunned that she would show up on his doorstep.

"I was about to shower," he said. He didn't want her in his house. He knew that once he saw her in it, the place would never be the same for him.

"This won't take long," she said crisply.

Cold air had moved in with the disappearing of the sun. It was too chilly to stand out on the front porch without a shirt. He realized there was no other choice but to invite her in.

Spencer stepped aside and held the door open for her. She breezed by him, head high, face set. Thoughtfully he stared after her, his hand absently rubbing his bare chest.

Once Jacqui was in the middle of the room, she whirled around to face him.

His eyes still on her, Spencer slowly reached back and shut the door. "So, what won't take long? I presume you came here to say something?"

The sound of his deep voice frustrated Jacqui even more. Her nostrils flared as she jammed her hands into the front pockets of her jeans.

"I came here," she said bitingly, "to tell you what an arrogant ass you are!"

Spencer moved away from the door. He could feel Jacqui's eyes measuring him up and down as he walked toward her.

"I admit that I should apologize for kissing you."

Her green eyes widened with outrage. "Apologize for kissing me! That's not—" She broke off, too angry to summon up any more words.

"You mean, the kiss isn't what made me an arrogant ass?" he taunted.

"No. I mean, yes. I mean—Spencer, you're making me madder!" She was close to shouting.

To her amazement he started to chuckle. She'd never seen him laugh about anything, and for a moment she forgot her anger and simply marveled at the change in him.

"Am I that amusing?" she wanted to know.

His laughter faded and he reached up and pushed long fingers through his hair.

"You're like a little red dust storm," he said.

There was no sarcasm in his voice now and Jacqui was suddenly aware that he was looking at her as a man looked at a woman. Her eyes slid over the heavy muscles of his shoulders and chest and arms. Golden-brown hair furred his chest while his flat belly was smooth and hard as it disappeared into the waistband of his jeans.

He was a sexy, virile-looking man. But he was also arrogant and complex. He was the kind of man that Jacqui wanted to avoid. Yet even so, a strange warmth curled in the pit of her stomach as she gazed at his lips. She wanted to kiss him again. Even though he obviously didn't like her, he didn't respect her, and he made her furious, she still wanted to feel his hard warm lips against hers, his strong arms around her, clasping her to him. The illogical desire was both confusing and frightening to Jacqui.

"What I meant," she repeated after taking a deep breath, "is that you should be apologizing for insulting me about Palmer Kirkland."

One side of his mouth cocked upward. "Why should I apologize for speaking the truth? Kirkland is a wolf and you're—"

He broke off and Jacqui stared at him.

"I'm what?" she prompted.

His eyes dropped from hers and he turned away and reached for an iron poker to stir up the fire.

"You're an attractive woman. A target for a man like him."

Jacqui watched him kneel down and shake up the burning logs. Sparks showered and flames leaped upward. His statement caught her off guard. It was the last thing she'd expected to hear him say. And what did it mean? That he might actually be concerned, maybe even jealous?

Some of the anger drained out of her. "Spencer," she said, the sting gone from her voice, "I've been working around men for some time now. I'm not naive to their ways."

He stood and turned to face her. She did her best to meet his gaze, but his bare chest was like a magnet drawing her eyes downward.

"Meaning what?" he asked.

"Meaning, even if Palmer Kirkland wanted me to ride for those reasons, I'd have more sense than to let him impress me in any way."

Spencer was relieved about that. "But still you want to ride for him," he persisted.

She lifted her hand, then let it fall to her side. "Of course I want to ride. I have to start somewhere."

He shook his head. "Why do you have to start at all? Why can't you be like other women?"

Spencer was mad at himself as soon as he allowed the words to slip out. She wouldn't understand how he felt and he didn't want to explain himself.

Jacqui's green eyes squinted on his handsome face. "Oh, so you're one of those kinds of men. I should have realized that a lot sooner."

"'One of those kinds of men,'" he repeated, hooking his thumbs on the front of his wide leather belt. "You've known a lot of men?"

Jacqui walked past him and stood with her back to the fire. "Like I told you, I've worked around a lot of men and several of them have been friends. But you, well, I must admit, Spencer, that I've never known a man quite like you."

"Am I supposed to take that as a compliment?"

"Please don't."

He grimaced. "Then what do you mean, Jacqui, by classifying me as 'one of those men'?"

She tossed her braid over her shoulder. "It means you think all women should stay in the kitchen. It means you think I'd be far better off if I were working with Gertrude."

His gaze dropped and Jacqui was aware that it was sliding over her breasts.

"Is something wrong with what Gertrude does?" he countered dryly.

"No. But then neither is there anything wrong with what I do," she staunchly defended.

"I see plenty wrong with it," he said, walking over to the couch. He sat down and began to tug off his muddy boots.

Jacqui wondered if there was anything else he planned to take off in front of her. "Like what? I only see it as a chosen profession."

He set his sharkskin boots to one side, then rested his forearms across his knees as he looked up at Jacqui. "Handling an eleven hundred pound horse traveling forty miles an hour around a dirt track is a man's job," he said, not bothering to elaborate.

She reached up with both hands and scraped the stray wisps of hair from her face. Her cheekbones were very prominent and even more now that they were splashed with pink color.

"I can handle a horse as well or better than any male jockey you know," she told him confidently. "My riding record proves it."

She was even worse than he first imagined, he thought. He rubbed a hand over his face. "I suppose you like being a rarity among all those men," he went on.

Jacqui almost wanted to laugh. Almost, but not quite. "Spencer, how old are you?"

"What?"

"I asked how old you were."

"Thirty-two. Why? Does my age interest you?"

She speared him with a mocking look. "I was just wondering how many years it took for you to grow into such a domineering, male chauvinist. You're the one who should have been named Bold Tyrant instead of that black colt down in the stables. It fits you perfectly."

He left the couch and crossed the space between them. Jacqui's head tilted up as she stared at his face. Mere inches separated them and Jacqui kept trying to focus on their conversation, but the memory of their kiss kept getting in the way.

"Jacqui, we're different people. It's not that I don't like you," he told her, surprising himself. For the past week he'd told himself over and over that he didn't like Jacqueline. But in spite of all his efforts, he still felt drawn to her.

"I see. You just go around insulting people you like. Is that it?" she asked.

"If my recollection is right, you've already managed to insult me several times."

Jacqui's mouth parted with surprise. "I haven't deliberately set out to insult you, as you have me."

"Let's see," he said pointedly. "There was 'arrogant ass,' 'domineering male chauvinist,' 'tyrant.' Have I left anything else out?"

Jacqui's face flamed with color. She'd never been a person who flung names and insults at people. She'd always tried to show people the kind of respect she wanted for herself. But that was just it, she thought, Spencer didn't respect her.

"If you had a good excuse for maligning me, Spencer, then I would apologize. But you don't. The only thing I can figure is that you resent my coming to Prescott Farms. So I'll go ahead and disappoint you further and tell you there's no chance I'll be leaving."

His eyes glinted down at her. She was a beautiful little bundle of life. Spencer knew that when she loved a man, it would be passionately. There would be no meekness or mildness about her, in or out of bed, his mind tacked on erotically.

"Did I say I wanted you to leave?" he drawled, his voice dropping to a soft, dangerous whisper.

Jacqui felt herself shiver even though the fire heated her back. This man was more than she bargained for both physically and mentally.

"You've said it in a thousand different ways," she murmured.

Spencer's insides tightened into a white-hot coil just begging to be released. Feeling like a hungry man, he bent his head toward her upturned face. "I don't resent your being here, Jacqui. I resent you being—" He stopped abruptly.

Needing to understand him, Jacqui prompted, "Being what?"

"Nothing," he answered huskily. He couldn't bring himself to tell her that he resented her for being like Danielle and like his mother.

His answer bewildered and frustrated her, but both of those emotions could not douse the temptation of his nearness. Her thinking grew cloudy and she felt her lids lower as if they were weighted.

"I don't know of anything about me that should bother you," she said, whispering now because his mouth was only a fraction of an inch from hers.

His hands slid around her waist and Jacqui suddenly felt as if she were in the midst of a deep, dark flame.

His mouth twisted wryly. "But there is, Jacqui. In fact, you bother the hell right out of me."

"Spencer—" His name came out part protest, part awe.

Spencer was tired of words—his and hers. He wanted to feel. He wanted her in his arms. He wanted her mouth on his. He wanted to absorb her softness, her warmth, her vibrancy. He wanted to hold on to her until the emptiness inside him was filled once again.

The wanting made him capture her mouth with reckless abandon. Jacqui groaned while her hands clutched his arms for support. She felt his hands draw her closer, then slip down her dusty jeans to splay across her bottom. Spencer tugged her hips up against his, lifting Jacqui off her feet.

She dangled helplessly against him, captured by his mouth and his arms. Her hands gripped the muscles covering his shoulders, even though she knew there was no danger of her falling. Spencer's strength surrounded her, making her acutely aware of his masculinity.

Strangely enough, Jacqui realized she liked being lost to him. She liked the feel of his naked chest against her, the taste of his mouth, the touch of his tongue and the sultry smell of his skin and hair. And she knew it showed in the way she clung to him, the way her lips responded to his kiss.

Jacqui's head was whirling, her breathing swift and shallow when Spencer finally lifted his mouth from hers. She looked at him drowsily, wondering why he had the power to make her behave so recklessly, so wantonly.

"Do you kiss every woman who bothers you?" she asked.

He smiled sensuously and he relaxed his arms, allowing her to slide slowly down the front of him. "You're the only woman who bothers me, Jacqui."

"There's nothing I can do about that," she said, knowing her cheeks were splashed with color. He was still holding her close to him and she was blatantly aware of his arousal. She was aware of her own arousal, too, and knew that it was dangerous to be this close to this man.

"Oh, yes, you could," he drawled. "You could tell me you won't ride tomorrow for Palmer Kirkland. There will be plenty of jockeys over at the track willing to take your mounts."

Jacqui felt sad as she pulled away from his grasp and turned her back to him. There was so much about Spencer that made her feel good, yet there was also the other side of him that troubled and angered her.

"I can't do that."

He shifted closer, curling his hands over her shoulders. Jacqui felt a part of her wilt inside at his warm touch.

"You mean you won't do it."

She breathed deeply. "Can't or won't, it makes no difference how I word it. The bottom line is I love to ride. It's what I've been trained to do. I'm sorry you can't accept that. We would make a good team, Spencer, you and I."

Jacqui turned and met the angry look in his brown eyes. "You're a good trainer," she went on. "And I'm a good rider. It's senseless to work at odds. I'd much rather win on your horses than on Palmer Kirkland's."

The anger lighting his eyes suddenly turned to sparks of pure fury. "I guess you think I'm like any other man," he spat out. "A couple of hot kisses and I'll fall at your feet and promise you anything. But, baby, that's not the way it works with me. Like I told you before, you'll never ride my horses!"

Jacqui was stung speechless. She couldn't believe the venom in his words. Anger and deep disappointment flooded through her. How could he possibly think she'd kissed him for that reason? Did he actually think she used physical favors to get mounts? The whole idea was unbearable.

"Oh, hell, there's no talking to you," she muttered, then whirled on her boot heel and headed quickly for the door. She was about to step onto the porch when she decided to look back at him. "But just for the record, it's none of your business who I ride for. And another thing, it's going to feel damn good when I beat you."

She slammed the door behind her, yet the sound didn't drown out Spencer's mocking snort. The man was crazy, and she was crazy for trying to deal with him. From now on she would stay far out of his way. And she'd be damned before she'd let him kiss her again!

Jacqui was shaking all over by the time she reached the house, but she was determined to get Spencer Matlock out of her mind. She took a quick bath, then slipped into a powder-blue sweater and straight skirt. After brushing her hair loose and dabbing on a few cosmetics, she went to find her uncle.

He was still in the study, working over a mound of papers. Jacqui knocked lightly at the open door, "Uncle Hadley?"

He looked up and smiled. "Need something, honey?"

"I just wanted to let you know I'm going into town. I'll get a snack there for supper. I'll tell Gertrude not to set a plate for me."

"What's the matter? Getting a little cabin fever?" He pulled off his reading glasses and rubbed his eyes.

Jacqui grimaced. No, not cabin fever, she thought. More like Spencer Matlock fever. "No, nothing like that," she answered. "I thought I'd pick up a racing form so I could study it before the race tomorrow. It will help to know what kind of horses I'll be running against."

He leaned back in his desk chair and smiled proudly at her. "I can't wait to see you ride tomorrow, Jacqui. And you can bet I'll be doing some bragging."

Jacqui shook her head. "I wouldn't say that too soon, Uncle Hadley. I might embarrass you."

"You could never do that, darlin'," he said with a shake of his head. "By the way, did you go see Spence?"

The smile fell from her face. "Yes, I did."

"And? Did you get things smoothed over between you?"

Jacqui felt her fingers gripping the door frame. "They're probably as smooth as they'll ever be between Spencer and me."

Hadley put his glasses back on and reached for another invoice. "It'll take time, Jacqui. Spencer will get used to having a woman around, and you'll grow to learn that he's actually a good man."

Good for training horses, but that was all, as far as Jacqui was concerned. "Yes, well, I hope you're right."

She went to the kitchen and told Gertrude about her plans, then drove the ten miles into town at a slow speed. She used the time to unwind, focusing her mind on the traffic and her driving instead of Spencer. By the time she reached the outskirts of town, she was feeling much better and looking forward to tomorrow's races.

Instead of driving on downtown, Jacqui stopped at a large convenience store that also served beverages and hot sandwiches. She'd stopped at the store several times since she'd come to live on Prescott Farms and she'd already become friends with a woman who worked the cash register.

Betty was there working when Jacqui pushed through the glass door. The woman was slightly plump, her hair was a shocking carrot red, and she had a pretty face and a warm smile. Jacqui had liked her the first time she met her.

"Well, hi, Jacqui," she said cheerfully. "You going out on the town? It's Friday night. A beautiful thing like you shouldn't be spending it alone."

Jacqui smiled and shook her head. She could have told Betty that she'd had enough of men for one evening. "I only came in for a racing form. Do you have any for tomorrow's races?"

"Sure thing." Betty reached behind her and handed the newspaper-type program to Jacqui. "What about something to eat? You need something to munch on while you read?"

Jacqui nodded. "A barbecue, Betty, and a cup of coffee."

"Won't be but a minute," the buxom redhead said.

Jacqui took a seat at one of the booths against the plate-glass windows and quickly buried her head in the racing form.

She would be riding in the third and the eleventh races. The eleventh was a Thoroughbred race at a distance of a mile and a quarter. The third was a quarter horse at four hundred yards. It was for the eleventh race that Jacqui required more knowledge about her mount. Did he start fast, was he a lead horse, or did he prefer to hang back and then make his move? Palmer Kirkland had said Stormin' Home had faded in the stretch his last race. Jacqui didn't want that to happen tomorrow.

The quarter horse she would be riding was a brown filly named Ima Easy Choice. From the looks of her past performances, she'd started slow from the gates, ended either three or four lengths from the winner.

Jacqui knew both horses would probably go off at a long odds on the betting board. They weren't exactly big winners by any means. But as she'd told Spencer, she had to start somewhere. There were times a good jockey could make a fair horse into a competitive one. Jacqui was confident of her skill, even if Spencer wasn't, she thought dismally.

"Here you go, Jacqui," Betty said, breaking into Jacqui's thoughts.

She looked up to see the woman placing her sandwich and coffee in front of her. "Thanks, Betty. Why don't you sit down and join me for a minute? There's no customers right now."

Betty plopped down on the bench opposite Jacqui and the two talked for a few minutes until Betty spied another customer at the counter. "Looks like I need to go back to work. I'll see you at the races," she tossed over her shoulder at Jacqui.

Jacqui finished her sandwich then studied the horses more thoroughly as she sipped her coffee.

An hour and a half later, she told Betty good-night and stepped outside. She'd almost forgotten her anger at Spencer. Tomorrow she would be racing again and the thought made her spirits soar.

While Claude had been at death's door, Jacqui hadn't taken on any mounts. So it had been some time since she'd competed. She was looking forward to it with eager excitement, one that even Spencer Matlock could not take away.

Jacqui was reaching for the handle on her car door when a pickup pulled up behind her. She glanced up to see it was black and loaded with chrome. She knew almost instantly that it was Spencer's.

Her heart thumped with anticipation as she waited for him to climb down from the truck. Jacqui wondered why she always reacted to his presence. He was just another man, she told herself. Another man with a cruel tongue.

She watched his tail form stride toward her. He'd changed from his work clothes into gray jeans and a black shirt. There was a lean, tough look about him that clothes could never disguise, she thought.

Spencer stopped within a few steps of her. His eyes flicked over her skirt and sweater then stopped on her face.

Jacqui's brows lifted as she met his gaze. He was smoking a cigarette, something she'd never seen him do before.

"Is something wrong back at the farm?" she asked.

He tugged his gray Stetson a bit farther down on his forehead. "It's getting late. Hadley was worried about you," he said shortly.

Hadley worried about her? That didn't make sense. From the time she'd come to live at Prescott Farms her uncle had treated her as an adult woman, fully capable of watching out for herself. She glanced at her wristwatch. "It's only nine o'clock," she commented.

"That's late enough when you have ten miles to drive back to the farm," he said.

He took a few steps closer and Jacqui eyed him with cool speculation. "Are you checking up on me, Spencer?"

He gave her a dry look. "Should I be?"

Jacqui gripped the racing form with both hands. "I suppose you thought I was having a rendezvous with Palmer Kirkland."

His expression stiffened, telling Jacqui that was exactly what he had thought. Disgusted, she turned to open her car door. "Sorry to prove you wrong. I only came in to town for a racing form," she told him.

Spencer felt relief flood through him as his eyes ran over her slender shoulders, tiny waist and the flare of her hips beneath the tight blue skirt. She had a sexy gracefulness about her, and even now it was so easy to remember the feel of her against him. He couldn't bear to think of another man touching her, even though he knew his possessiveness was illogical.

"I had a racing form at home. If you'd only asked, I would have gone over it with you," he said.

Jacqui looked back at him. Amazement parted her lips and widened her eyes. "Why would I ask you for help?"

"I know most of the horses you'll be running against tomorrow."

Jacqui turned back to the car and proceeded to open the door. "You probably do," she told him. "But so do I—now."

Spencer didn't want her riding for Palmer Kirkland, and he certainly didn't want her to turn to him or some other man for advice. But he couldn't tell Jacqui that. He didn't even want to admit it to himself.

"I'll follow you home," he said gruffly, dropping his cigarette butt and grinding it with his boot heel. "And I expect you to obey the speed limits."

Jacqui wanted to groan with frustration, but instead she gritted her teeth and said nothing. She felt more than saw him watching her as she slid beneath the wheel and started the engine of her little car.

Spencer followed her closely all the way back to the farm. Jacqui was unnerved by his presence. Throughout the drive, she kept going over his words, trying to figure him out. But she eventually decided that figuring out Spencer was impossible. He was too complex and she was too vulnerable to him to make any sense of their battles.

When Jacqui braked to a stop at the main house, she fully expected Spencer to pull in beside her. However, his pickup kept going on the track that led to his house.

Jacqui let out a thankful breath then hurried into the house. She found Hadley in the living room watching a TV program. He looked up with mild interest as Jacqui appeared in the room.

"Have a good evening, darlin'?"

Jacqui's forehead wrinkled with confusion. Spencer had said Hadley was worried about her. This didn't look or sound like a worried man.

"It was fine, until Spencer showed up," she said truthfully.

Hadley turned his attention away from the TV to look at her. "Spence showed up where? I thought you were in town?"

Jacqui went very still. "I was. But then Spencer showed up just about the time I was leaving. He said you were worried about me."

Hadley folded his arms across his broad chest as a speculative smile spread across his face. "Worried, huh? Well, darlin', I think you can take care of yourself. Spencer just happened to come over and I mentioned you'd been in town a couple of hours. I never said I was worried, though."

Jacqui's mouth opened then promptly closed. She didn't know what Spencer had been up to, but obviously he hadn't come to town searching for her on Hadley's behalf. So what did that mean? That he was checking up on her himself? The whole idea left her with a strange feeling.

"Why, what's the matter, honey? You and Spence didn't get into it again, did you?"

Jacqui looked at her uncle, but actually her mind was picturing Spencer and the look on his face as he'd bent to kiss her.

"Uh, no. We didn't have another fight. I just simply obeyed him to avoid having one."

Hadley chuckled under his breath. "Don't give in on my account, Jacqui. You handle Spencer any way you want to."

The idea of "handling" Spencer was overwhelming to Jacqui to say the least.

"I'll think about that, Uncle. But right now I believe I'll turn in. I want to be rested for the races tomorrow."

"Why don't you tell Spencer you don't want to gallop the horses in the morning? I'm sure J.T. can handle it."

Jacqui shook her head. "No way. The ponies would think I've deserted them." Not to mention that Spencer would say she was sloughing off because she was Hadley's niece, she thought grimly. "Good night, Uncle Hadley."

"Good night, Jacqui."

By the time Jacqui entered her bedroom she decided she didn't give a damn what Spencer Matlock thought about her. The horses on this place might have to bow to his hand, but as far as she was concerned, she never would.

Chapter Four

Blue Ribbon Downs was situated west of Sallisaw and close to I-40. The racetrack had grown immensely, Hadley had told Jacqui, since pari-mutuel wagering had been voted in by the state.

The day of the races, Jacqui chose to drive her own car to the track instead of riding with Spencer and Hadley. A sunny, azure sky stretched across the hills and rolling prairies surrounding Sallisaw. She was pleased about the beautiful weather. A muddy track slowed the horses and greatly increased the chance of crippling an animal. But today the track would be dry and fast.

Jacqui was pleased when she saw the track for the first time. The facilities were beautiful, modern and well maintained. It was different from Ruidoso in that both quarter horses and Thoroughbreds ran on the same track. But that didn't bother Jacqui because she knew the track was thoroughly resurfaced after each race.

Prescott Farms had two horses racing today. When Jacqui had left home, Hadley and Spencer were busy wrapping the horses' legs and loading them into the trailer for the ride over to the track.

She felt a pang of sadness, knowing she wouldn't be riding the two horses. Claude would have been so pleased to know that she was jockeying for Prescott Farms.

But Jacqui didn't want to ride Prescott's horses only because she was a relative of Hadley and Claude. She wanted to ride them because Spencer trusted her as a good, competent jockey. And since that wasn't the case, she knew such a wish was impossible. Spencer would never see fit to allow her to ride.

In spite of all that, Jacqui was in high spirits when she arrived at the track. She went straight to the jockey's quarters, weighed and signed in with the clerk of scales. Jacqui discovered there were a few women jockeys who rode from time to time at Blue Ribbon Downs. In fact one would be riding today, so Jacqui wouldn't be a rarity.

Between races, a jockey was confined to the jockey quarters situated upstairs over the saddling paddock. While Jacqui waited there for her own race, she watched the first two races on a monitor, then went to the dressing room to change into her riding silks, a dark blue top over white pants.

After she'd pulled on her black boots and secured her long hair with a black ribbon, she grabbed up her helmet and batting quirt and hurried down to the

saddling paddock. She was anxious to ask Palmer
Kirkland how the horse seemed to be feeling.

The saddling stalls were situated inside a huge
building connected to the grandstands, so the spectators could watch the horses being saddled prior to each
race.

As Jacqui pushed through the glass double doors
that led to the paddock, she noticed there was a tre-
mendous crowd today. People gathered along the ce-
ment wall that separated the horses' area from the
spectators.

She walked over the clean wood shavings with her
helmet and goggles under her left arm and her bat
swinging in her right hand. She searched for Hadley
or Spencer, but she saw neither one. She supposed
they were both still over at the haul-in barns tending
to the horses.

Palmer Kirkland was a tall, black-haired man with
a thick walrus mustache. He was nice-looking on the
outside, Jacqui decided, but he didn't attract her in the
way Spencer did. Maybe that was too bad, she thought
bitterly. At least Palmer treated her as though she had
some common sense about her.

"Hello, Jacqui," he said with a wide smile. "Ready
to ride?"

She nodded, her eyes quickly going to the filly he
was holding. "Very ready. How is Ima Easy Choice
feeling today?"

Palmer ran his hand down the filly's sleek neck. She
responded with a snort and a lunge on the bits. "She's
on a high right now. But whether she can keep up with
the rest of the pack is anyone's guess."

There was a man standing to Palmer's right, whom Jacqui quickly decided was Ima Easy Choice's owner. She looked at him and smiled.

He extended his hand. "I'm Charles Grayson," the older man introduced himself. "Palmer tells me you're a good jockey."

Jacqui shook his hand. "Mr. Kirkland doesn't know, yet," she said with a joking laugh. "But I assure you I want to win as badly as you do."

The starter was signaling for the number one horse to leave its stall. Jacqueline settled her helmet on her head and prepared to mount. It was race time and adrenaline was surging through her.

This would be her first performance here and she prayed it would be respectable. The crowd would be watching, and so would Spencer.

"We really shouldn't have come over here," Spencer barked at Hadley as the horses began to come out on the track. The two men were standing against the fence. "Our race is only two races away. We're going to be late getting to the saddling paddock."

"We can make it," Hadley said with a calmness that grated on Spencer's nerves.

Spencer gritted his teeth and reached for a cigarette. The track announcer was introducing the horses and Jacqui was next in line.

"The number three horse is Ima Easy Choice with Jacqueline Prescott in the irons."

Spencer didn't hear anything else as he watched Jacqui and Palmer ride by. She was smiling and talking with the man, appearing as relaxed as if she were going for an afternoon ride in the park.

The sight made Spencer furious. He hated that it was Palmer Kirkland beside her instead of himself. He knew it was foolish to have such a possessive feeling toward Jacqui. But he had to admit the feeling was there just the same, no matter how hard he tried to push it away.

Spencer took a drag off his cigarette, then threw it down and ground it out beneath his boot. He couldn't breathe, he couldn't swallow, his palms were clammy and his heart was like a runaway freight train in his chest. He didn't know what was coming over him. He only knew that Jacqui was causing this change. And he hated her for doing it, for making him see her as a beautiful, desirable woman.

"Spencer, are you getting sick?" Hadley asked.

Spencer turned to see the older man eyeing him with a concerned look. "No, why do you ask?"

"You look like you've stuck your head in a flour bin. Are you sure you're feeling okay?"

"I—it's just a little headache," he said. "I'm all right."

The horses were entering the gates now. Hadley lifted his binoculars to his eyes. Spencer stood there squinting down at the far end of the track, and silently cursing Hadley for making him come over to watch Jacqui's race.

"She's loaded," Hadley said, then handed the field glasses out to Spencer. "Here, look for yourself."

"I can see her like this! That damn filly will rear up in the gates. I've seen her do it before!"

Hadley frowned and looked through the glasses again. "She's standing perfectly still, Spencer."

"Kirkland damn well better hold her still, or he'll answer to me!" Spencer said through gritted teeth.

The next moment the flag was up and the gates popped. The announcer's voice boomed out, "They're off!"

"Hot damn, Spence! She's jumped out in the lead!" Hadley exclaimed.

"She'll fade."

"She's not gonna fade. She's gonna win this thing!" Hadley shouted with glee.

Spencer watched the horses flying up the track while his heart pounded in his throat. As they neared the last hundred yards, he could see Jacqui tight against the filly's neck and batting the horse's hindquarters for all she was worth. She was a half length ahead of the number six horse.

He'd never seen Palmer's filly run this fast. The horse's speed surprised him. But realizing he was concerned for Jacqui's safety stunned him much more.

With a transfixed stare, Spencer watched the horses roar across the finish line.

"He caught her! The number six horse nipped her at the wire!" Hadley bellowed with disappointment.

"It was too close to call," Spencer said, aware that his voice was hoarse.

It was difficult for Spencer to think about the outcome of the race at all. He was still thinking about his concern for Jacqui. Concern meant caring, didn't it? He couldn't let himself care for Jacqui, he thought desperately. Women like her could only be counted on for two things—pain and heartache.

The trainers were standing out on the track between the tote board and the winner's circle, waiting for the horses to return.

Jacqui pulled the filly to a stop, then waved her bat, giving the signal to the stewards that she was not fouled during the race.

"I'm sorry, Mr. Kirkland," she said, tossing the bat down to him, then jumping down from the saddle. "That six horse got us. But—"

"Sorry!" Palmer exclaimed, "Jacqui, I couldn't be happier. You put some ride on this filly! She's never finished this well before."

Jacqui glanced up at the tote board to see the word "photo." However, she didn't need a photo to know the winner. Even so, she was extremely proud to register second place.

"She's a good filly. She jumped well from the gates. And I didn't feel her tiring until the last yard or two," she said.

The crowd began to yell and whistle as the winners were posted on the board. Jacqui began uncinching the saddle so that she could weigh in with the rest of the jockeys.

"I'll see you later, Jacqui," Palmer called to her as she walked off the track.

She glanced over her shoulder to see him giving her a broad smile. She smiled back at him, not in a flirting way, but just to say thanks for giving her this chance. It was more than Spencer had done, she thought sadly.

Spencer's horses were running in the fifth and ninth races. One placed second, the other third. Which were nothing to be ashamed of since both were in very tough races.

When Jacqui rode her mount out on the track for the eleventh race, she spotted Hadley and Spencer standing near the fence at the finish line. Hadley gave her a big thumbs-up sign. Spencer merely gave her a cool glance.

Palmer said, "I don't mean to be nosy, Jacqui, but why aren't you riding Prescott horses?"

She felt herself blushing. "A difference of opinion between me and the trainer, you might say."

"Oh." He looked thoughtful for a moment. "Spencer is a good trainer. Everyone around here knows that. But he's a private person. When you're around him, you never really know what he's thinking."

Jacqui took a deep breath and clutched the reins in her hands. "I think Stormin' Home needs to be held back until the half-mile marker," she said, determined to bring the subject back to the race at hand. "Otherwise, I believe he'll tire."

"You're the jockey, Jacqui. Whatever you think, I'll go along with."

Jacqui nodded, silently hoping she'd guessed right about the big, red Thoroughbred.

"I've overheard several of the men talking about Jacqui's ride," Hadley said proudly as he and Spencer waited for the race to start. "If she makes a good showing on this horse, the phone will be ringing off the wall with offers for her to ride."

Spencer suddenly felt like cursing. "I don't understand why you told Kirkland about Jacqui anyway. You know how he is around women!"

Hadley looked at him questioningly. "How he is around women? I thought Jacqui was riding his horses, not going out on a date with the man."

"I'm sure that will come next," Spencer growled.

"Jacqui's smart enough to pick the good ones from the bad ones." He glanced at Spencer's brooding expression. "You really don't want her to ride at all, do you, Spencer? Or is it like Jacqui believes, you just don't like her?"

Spencer was suddenly seeing Jacqui's face. Her warm smiles, the flash of her green eyes. Feeling definitely uncomfortable, he tugged at his hat brim, then met the appraising look in Hadley's eyes. "Hadley, I know that she's your niece. And I...I admit she's very good with horses. But—"

"But what?" Hadley prompted.

Spencer heaved out a frustrated breath. "I heard she divorced her husband," he said before he could change his mind about broaching the subject with Hadley.

"Damn right, she divorced him," Hadley snorted with conviction. "If she hadn't divorced him I would have gone out to Ruidoso and shook some sense into her myself."

"If she hadn't divorced him." Hadley's words echoed through Spencer's head. He looked blankly at Hadley. "What do you mean? I thought after you lost Emma, you despised the word divorce. Are you saying you wanted Jacqui to divorce her husband?"

"Me, Claude, and anyone else who cared about Jacqui," he said as he raised the binoculars to his eyes and focused on the horses. "That sorry thing she was married to—"

The horses bolted from the starting gates and Hadley left the sentence unfinished.

Stunned by what Hadley had just implied, Spencer gripped the iron railing in front of him. All along he'd thought Jacqui was the guilty party in the breakup of her marriage.

Grim-faced, Spencer turned his attention to the race, while telling himself he was definitely going to find out about Jacqui's past one way or the other.

Both men watched in silence as the pack of ten clipped around the first turn of the track. When the horses approached the second turn, Jacqui was third from the last, while the leader was a good two lengths ahead of the pack.

Hadley said, "What is she doing?"

"She's saving him," Spencer said, his eyes riveted on Jacqui.

"I don't know about saving him that much," Hadley said doubtfully. The horses were in the back stretch, nearing the half-mile marker. Stormin' Home was beginning to make his move.

He passed one horse, then two. By the time they reached the third turn, he was running in the middle of the horses. Rounding the last turn, Jacqui made her move on the outside and turned Stormin' Home loose.

Hadley began to grin. Spencer merely watched as Jacqui started to put the bat to Stormin' Home's hindquarters. Once he passed the lead horse it was all over. The big sorrel stretched out to finish a good four lengths ahead of the pack.

Hadley was exuberant. He threw his hat in the air and did a jig. The crowd roared as Stormin' Home, which had gone off at twenty-five to one odds, was posted as the winner. The pari-mutuel tickets would pay off big on this race.

"Let's get down to the winner's circle and get in the win picture," Hadley told Spencer.

Spencer shook his head. "Not with one of Kirkland's horses," he said.

Hadley started to argue, then deciding against it, he turned and walked away.

Spencer stood there watching the older man wedging his way through the thick crowd to congratulate his niece.

To say that Spencer had mixed emotions when Palmer Kirkland led Jacqui and Stormin' Home into the winner's circle would have been a gross understatement. On one hand, he was very happy for her. She'd proved to him how well she knew horses and that she was an excellent jockey. On the other hand, it actually hurt him to see her with Kirkland, to know that she was sharing this victory with someone else. He didn't understand any of his feelings. He only knew he'd never felt more miserable and alone.

As Jacqui entered the circle she instantly spotted Hadley, then just as quickly realized that Spencer was not with him.

Lifting her head, Jacqui quickly scanned the crowd and saw him standing several yards away, watching her. For long moments they looked at each other. Jacqui smiled at him, but he did not smile back. Instead he lifted a forefinger to the brim of his hat as if to say, "You won, I accede, but I don't like it."

Jacqui's heart was suddenly very heavy and the feeling confused her. This should have been one of the happiest moments of her life. Instead Spencer was spoiling it for her.

"Now entering the winner's circle for today's eleventh race," the track announcer stated, "is Stormin' Home. The sorrel gelding is owned by Charles Grayson of Fort Smith, Arkansas, and trained by Palmer Kirkland. Stormin' Home was ridden to victory by Jacqueline Prescott. The official time for the race was 1:46."

Jacqui took off her helmet and smiled at the camera. Beneath her, the horse, still fired up from his run, snorted and danced impatiently. Around her, people were congratulating each other. Among the noise, she picked up Hadley's voice.

"Great ride, darlin'. I'm proud of you!"

"Thanks, Uncle Hadley." After the photographer snapped the last picture, Jacqui slid to the ground, then stepped over to give her uncle a hug.

"Jacqui, from now on there will never be anyone but you on my horses," Palmer Kirkland spoke up behind her. "I never dreamed that horse would have late speed like he showed."

Jacqui turned to Palmer and smiled happily. "He was still straining against the bits when we crossed the finish line. He's a wonderful horse."

Palmer smiled back at her. "I'd say you're a wonderful jockey. I'd love to buy you a steak dinner, in appreciation," he added.

Jacqui opened her mouth to decline at the same time Hadley spoke up. "My niece has already made plans to eat with me and Spencer."

"Oh. Well maybe next time, Jacqui," Palmer suggested.

She said, "Maybe," then took the saddle from him and headed to the scales. "I'd better weigh in. The security guards are ready to escort the jockeys back into the building."

Back in the dressing room, Jacqui changed into her black jeans and black-and-white striped blouse, brushed her hair, and dabbed on a bit of makeup.

By the time she was finished, the twelfth and last race for the day was over. People were already beginning to file out of the club house and the grandstands.

Jacqui walked across the concrete parking area to her little white car. To her surprise, Hadley was waiting for her.

"Aren't you helping Spencer with the horses?" she asked.

"They're already taken care of. I told Spence we'd meet him at the steak house."

Jacqui was quite sure she didn't want to sit across a table from Spencer and endure his snide remarks. "I'm not that hungry, Uncle."

"Nonsense," he said, waving away her words. "You've put in a hard day's work. Or would you rather have had supper with Palmer Kirkland?"

Jacqui, who was unlocking the car door, lifted her head to look at her uncle. "No."

"Good, that's why I opened my mouth like I did. I'm glad I didn't guess wrong."

A faint smile touched Jacqui's mouth at Hadley's concern. "I'm grateful to Palmer Kirkland for giving me the chance to ride his horses. But other than that, he doesn't interest me."

"I didn't think for a minute that he did," Hadley said with a knowing little grin.

Jacqui slid behind the steering wheel, then unlocked the passenger side so that Hadley could join her.

The steak house Hadley had referred to was only a couple of miles away. Once they were out of the bumper-to-bumper traffic leaving the racetrack, Jacqui covered the distance in no time.

Spencer was standing outside his truck and trailer waiting when Jacqui pulled into the parking lot. The three of them went inside, found a table by the window, and placed their orders.

Jacqui sipped her coffee quietly as the two men talked over the races. But then suddenly Hadley spotted an old friend and left her and Spencer alone together.

Jacqui wondered if her uncle had deliberately thrown her and Spencer together. If she thought for a minute that he had, Jacqui would certainly talk to him about it.

Across the table, Spencer lifted his water glass. "I should congratulate you, Jacqui, you put in two good rides today."

Jacqui knew it was costing him to say such a thing to her, and she met his eyes. There was a pale, strained look on his face, one that Jacqui had never seen before.

"Thank you, Spencer." It was all she felt compelled to say.

Spencer studied her beneath lowered lashes. He couldn't understand why she wasn't lowering the boom, rubbing her victory in on him. "Is that all, just a thank-you?"

Jacqui's brows lifted. "What else would you like to hear? Except that your horses did very well. I think the Thoroughbred wasn't positioned very well. Maybe you should talk to your jockey about that."

Jacqui was right. He hadn't been ridden very well, so Spencer said nothing.

Jacqui shifted uncomfortably on the padded seat and wished that Hadley would return. She looked across the room to her uncle, and her spirits sank as she saw the waitress serving his meal at the other table.

The waitress walked across the room until she reached Spencer and Jacqui. She served Spencer a rare rib eye, then placed a plate of boneless chicken in front of Jacqui and refilled their coffee cups. Jacqui wasn't hungry, but at least the food would give her something to do.

"Hadley seems to think you'll have no trouble getting rides now. Especially with people knowing you've settled here close to the track," Spencer said.

Jacqui chewed a bite of chicken. She kept her eyes on her plate instead of him. It was safer that way. "Maybe. I guess you hate that idea."

Spencer let out a deep sigh. There was a strained sound to her voice. He suddenly realized he didn't want to hurt her. He'd never really wanted to hurt her, he'd just wanted to keep her at arm's length. "Jacqui, I—I know that your riding is none of my business.''

His admission surprised her so much that she lifted her head to look at him. "Are you trying to say something to me?"

He shrugged. "Just what I said. If you ride for Palmer Kirkland, or anyone else, it's nothing to me."

Jacqui gripped her fork. His words shouldn't hurt, but they did. It didn't make sense. She wanted him to care. She wanted whatever concerned her to matter to him. Oh, Jacqui, she thought dismally, what is happening to you? Why are you letting this man affect you?

She let out a jerky breath. "I do plan on riding more. I'm hoping that I'll soon be racing each day from Thursday through Sunday."

Spencer's eyes fell to his plate as he sliced his steak. "I don't want to fight with you, Jacqui. I don't like the idea of your racing, but I don't want to fight with you."

Jacqui's heart turned over. She didn't know just what he was offering, she only knew it was much more than she'd ever expected from him. "I don't want to fight with you, either, Spencer," she said carefully. "We have the same common interest. I wish we could be . . . be friends," she finished.

Spencer's mouth curved wryly. She hadn't kissed him like a friend, and that wasn't all he wanted from Jacqui. He knew that now. He did want her friendship and her kisses. "I'd like that, too, Jacqui," he said quietly.

Jacqui felt as if dark clouds had disappeared from the sky. Everything suddenly looked bright and beautiful, even the food on her plate. She dug into it with renewed hunger.

"You know, before Uncle Claude died he kept saying how much he wanted me to come here to Prescott Farms. I wanted to shout at him that there was no place like Ruidoso." She smiled wanly. "But I'm beginning to change my mind. I couldn't imagine having a nicer home than Prescott Farms and the track at Blue Ribbon Downs is far more than I'd ever expected."

Spencer reached for his coffee. Taking a sip, he eyed her closely. It was obvious that her uncle's death had been a traumatic loss to her. Not until the past week or two had she been able to say his name without getting tears in her eyes. He was glad to see she was putting that behind her now. He was even glad she considered this her home now. "You can always go back there for a visit," he suggested.

She laughed softly. "Or maybe for the All American Futurity. Now that would be a reason to go back for."

"Hadley is crazy about having you here with him," Spencer commented.

"Uncle Hadley is a kind, wonderful person. I adore him."

She met Spencer's gaze. The burgundy-colored shirt he was wearing made his skin look darker and his brown eyes browner. Jacqui felt giddy and weak every time she looked at him, especially now that he'd kissed her. She knew what it was like to be close to him, and she couldn't get it out of her mind.

"Have you trained racehorses for a long time?" she asked.

Spencer nodded. "Over ten years. I've lived on Prescott Farms a long time."

"Did you know Hadley's wife?"

"Yes. She was a different person than Hadley. They had absolutely nothing in common. She wanted to live back east and Hadley didn't. They eventually divorced. She lives in New York City now."

Jacqui shrugged. "I never mention her to Uncle Hadley. I was afraid it might be a touchy subject."

Spencer shook his head. "Not anymore. That was all a long time ago. He's gotten over it."

Jacqui's eyes followed the smooth lines of his face. She wanted to ask, What about you, Spencer, have you gotten over the loss of your wife? Yet she couldn't bring herself to say anything like that to him. He was a man who kept his distance.

And God help the woman inside her, she thought. The one who wanted to get closer to him, the one who wanted him to open his heart to her.

Spencer fixed his eyes on her face. "What about you, Jacqui?" he asked lowly. "Have you gotten over divorcing your husband?"

Chapter Five

Jacqui's whole body went rigid. "How did you know I was once married?" she asked, narrowing her eyes suspiciously on his face.

It was something she didn't talk about to anyone. It was in her past, something long dead. She couldn't imagine why Spencer should question her about it now.

"I just do," he said off-handedly. It didn't matter where he'd heard it. What mattered was the truth, and something inside Spencer was driving him to find it.

Jacqui grimaced. "It's not something I like to talk about," she told him, hoping he'd have the decency to drop the subject. It had been a humiliating experience, one that she didn't like to be reminded of.

"I'll just bet," he said dryly.

Sudden anger flared like a flame inside Jacqui. "What does that mean?"

Pretending indifference, Spencer shrugged. "I heard you divorced your husband. I also heard he was a struggling racehorse trainer."

Jacqui's teeth ground together as she reached for her coffee cup. "You heard right. On both counts."

For a moment she thought she saw a shadow of disappointment cross his face, as though he'd been hoping she would deny his words. The whole idea puzzled Jacqui even more.

"You mean you have no regrets, no guilt about leaving your husband?"

There was no mistaking the accusation in his voice. Jacqueline's temper soared. She longed to shout what a swine he was, but the diners sitting around them prevented it. Frustrated, she glanced around her, then back to Spencer.

"This is none of your business, Spencer," she ground out.

He leaned toward her, bringing his set, angry face within inches of hers.

"Just like I first thought," he flung back in a voice only for her ears. "You deserted him because he couldn't give you everything you wanted! You didn't have enough love or loyalty to stand beside him."

Jacqui gasped. "Is that what you think? Is that what you've been thinking about me all along?" she asked, completely shocked.

He didn't answer immediately. He didn't have to. Jacqui already knew the answer. Tears unexpectedly burned her eyes and all she could think of was getting out of the restaurant and away from Spencer.

The fork dropped from her hand and clattered loudly as it hit the tabletop. Quickly she pushed her chair back, but before she could get to her feet, Spencer caught hold of her. Jacqui looked down at his strong fingers wrapped around her wrist.

"Jacqui, please. What am I supposed to think? You didn't try to deny my words."

His voice was gentle, almost pleading. It surprised Jacqui, and she felt herself easing back into her chair in spite of her anger.

She raised her eyes back to his face. "I shouldn't have to justify myself to you!" she said in a low, fierce tone. "The past weeks we've worked together should be enough for you to see that I'm not that kind of person!"

There was hurt on her face, in her eyes. Spencer was struck by the sight of it, so much so that he couldn't bring himself to drop his hold on her wrist.

"You have to understand, Jacqui. Trusting and believing in people doesn't come easy for me. And when I heard you were the one who initiated the divorce and that you'd obviously taken back your maiden name—"

"Of course I took back my maiden name!" she shot back at him before he could finish. "I didn't want myself associated with Jay and—"

Jacqui suddenly stopped when his fingers released her wrist and his hand covered hers. Her eyes dropped to the tabletop and she swallowed as she struggled to calm herself.

"Spencer," she began again, "it's no secret that my husband was lacking morals. Everyone in Ruidoso knew it except me. When you called him a struggling trainer, you were right in one sense. He was struggling to keep several girlfriends in tow while his wife worked down at the track to pay the utility bills and put food on the table. He wasn't interested in succeeding as a trainer. He was more interested in women and spending the savings I'd made racing.''

Remorse swamped Spencer. The idea that he'd been so wrong about her, and then held it against her, made him sick inside. "Jacqui, I . . . I didn't know."

"Obviously," she said dryly, lifting her gaze back to him.

His hand tightened on hers. "I'm sorry for . . . misjudging you, Jacqui. I know that probably doesn't mean much to you but—"

It meant very much to Jacqui. Much more than he could possibly know. "Let's just forget it," she interrupted. "All of that was just one of those hard lessons of life. I've put it behind me now."

Spencer looked at his fingers still curled over hers. "There is one more thing I'd like to know," he said.

"What is that?" she asked a bit guardedly.

He looked back up at her. "Why did you marry a man like him in the first place?"

A wry smile touched her mouth. "I was only eighteen when I met Jay. I didn't see any further than his charm and his promises. Later I learned it had all been pretense on his part. It was a painful lesson."

Spencer released her hand and leaned back in his chair. He was very sorry that he'd more or less accused Jacqui of things she'd never been guilty of doing. But on the other hand, he suddenly felt glad about what he'd just learned from her.

She wasn't like his mother or Danielle, and knowing that lifted a heavy burden from his heart.

Much to Jacqui's relief, Spencer turned the conversation to lighter things. They were almost finished with their meal when Hadley returned to their table and informed them he was going with his friend to look at a horse that was for sale.

Jacqui followed Spencer home, driving slowly behind his pickup and trailer.

Throughout the drive, she kept thinking about Spencer's change of heart and what had prompted it. His whole attitude puzzled her. But that was really nothing new, she decided. The man had confused her from the first time she'd set foot on Prescott Farms.

Now that she had time to think about it, she was glad Spencer had brought up her marriage. It cleared up a lot of things that had bewildered her. His condescending attitude toward her, the way he'd virtually bristled at her that first day they met. He must have believed she was a woman who played fast and loose with men.

Maybe now that he knew the truth, she thought hopefully, things would be different between them.

Spencer had given David and Ken the remainder of the afternoon off. After Jacqui parked her car in front of the house, she walked down to the stables to see if she could help Spencer with the horses.

She found him in the barn, measuring out feed in a bucket. "Is there something I can help you with?" she asked as she walked up to him.

The sound of her voice surprised Spencer. His head jerked up to see her standing only a few feet away. "Filling the hay mangers is all that's left to do. I can manage," he answered.

Jacqui walked over to the stacked hay at the end of the barn and gathered up an armful. "It's getting very cold outside now that the sun has gone down," she commented. "Would you like to come up to the house and have a cup of coffee in front of the fireplace?"

"We just had coffee," Spencer said.

Without turning to look at him, Jacqui dropped the hay in the manger. "Yes. We did," she replied.

He led a horse into the stall next to where Jacqui stood.

She didn't know what to think of his curt response. Maybe she should have never made the invitation. Just because he'd said he wanted to be friends didn't necessarily mean he wanted to spend extra time with her.

"I have a fireplace, too, you know," he said after he'd slipped the halter off the horse's head.

"Yes, I remember," she said, even more unsure of what he was getting around to.

He led another horse into its stall and Jacqui went about the job of filling the second hay manger.

"Do you like apple cider?"

His question couldn't have surprised her more, yet she tried not to let him know this. "Yes, I do. You can buy great cider in the Hondo Valley near Ruidoso."

Jacqui followed him out of the stall. Spencer bolted the door shut, then hung the halter he was holding on a nearby hook.

"You can get great cider around here, too. If you'd like to come up to the house, you could try a cup."

Jacqui smiled warmly at him, happy that he wasn't snubbing her after all. "I'd like that."

A dimple appeared at the side of his mouth as he watched her brush the loose hay from her striped shirt. "You should be wearing a jacket."

"I left it at the house," she told him.

"I didn't expect you to come down here and help me. You're not a hired hand."

She shrugged. "David and Ken are off. And I like taking care of the horses."

They both started walking toward the end door, which led outside.

"You really love horses, don't you."

It was more a statement than a question. Jacqui warmed to it. "Very much. Even the difficult ones."

"My wife hated horses. Everything about them. Mostly I think she hated them because I loved them," Spencer said.

Jacqui remained silent as they walked along. She would have never expected him to mention his wife. The fact that he had momentarily stunned her. She wondered if he knew just how much he'd just told her with that one statement.

"Some people are, well, they're just not animal lovers," she said, making an effort to keep her voice light. "Now take me, I love anything that walks on four legs and has a hairy coat."

Spencer smiled faintly at her comment. She was very different from Danielle. He knew it even more now that she'd told him about her divorce. "Does that include rats?"

Jacqui laughed softly. "Well, uh, that might be taking things too far."

It was a slight uphill climb to Spencer's house. Jacqui hugged her arms about her to ward off the chilly wind.

On the porch, Spencer quickly grabbed up an armload of firewood and allowed Jacqui to precede him into the house.

Once inside, he invited her to have a seat, then quickly went about building a fire. Jacqui settled herself on the couch and looked around the room.

Yesterday she'd been too angry to notice her surroundings. Tonight she could see the living room connected with a dining area, and beyond that she guessed would be the kitchen. There was nothing frilly or fancy about the place, but it was very clean. There were Indian woven rugs scattered on the hardwood floor and one whole wall was covered with racing photos. Along the opposite wall was a long cedar chest with a kerosene lamp sitting on top of it. Other than the couch, a rolltop desk, and a stuffed armchair, there was no other furniture in the room.

Jacqui knew that Spencer made a good salary, so the lack of furniture couldn't be from a lack of money. Somehow she got the feeling that to Spencer, the house was just that—a house and not a home.

"I don't expect we'll have much more cold weather now. March is halfway through," Spencer spoke up as he stuck a long match to a piece of pine kindling.

"That will be good on the new foals being born," Jacqui said.

Spencer straightened, and Jacqui watched him as he took off his Stetson and placed it on the desk. His sandy hair was flattened against his forehead. With long fingers, he raked the hair back from his face, then looked over to Jacqui.

Spencer studied her for long moments until finally Jacqui shifted in her seat and blushed. "Is something wrong? Do I have a smudge on my nose?"

He shook his head. "I've never had a woman in this house. It seems strange to see you here."

Jacqui was floored by his statement. Surely the man entertained women from time to time! After all, he was a young, red-blooded male.

"I can't believe that. Surely your wife—"

"We didn't live here. I moved into this house after she was killed."

He said the words unemotionally, but Jacqui got the impression that underneath his passive attitude were feelings no one knew about. "Hadley told me she'd been killed in a car accident. It must have been shocking and terrible for you."

He gave one nod. "Yes. It was."

She pushed back a wave of hair that had fallen against her face and looked at him through lowered lashes. "Tell me about her. Was she beautiful?"

He grimaced slightly. "She wasn't exactly beautiful. More like flamboyant. She was blond and much taller than you. She was—" He paused thoughtfully, then suddenly a tightness settled over his features and he said rather brusquely, "She liked to live fast. And that was the way she died."

Jacqui swallowed, not liking to think of Spencer going through the pain of losing a loved one. She remembered Gertrude saying he'd never been the same man since. Jacqui wondered in what way.

"I suppose she died before you had the chance to have children."

Spencer didn't reply and Jacqui watched the color drain from his face.

"Danielle didn't want children," he said after a moment.

Jacqui realized she'd treaded on sensitive ground. "I—I'm sorry. I was prying."

Embarrassed, she rose to her feet and nervously rubbed her hands down the front of her jeans. "Are you ready for that cider? If you'll show me where things are, I'll heat it for us."

He motioned his head toward the dining area. "The kitchen is through there."

Jacqui walked quickly ahead of him. The kitchen was small and felt even smaller when Spencer followed her into it. She was so aware of him that she could think of nothing else.

He pulled out a jug of cider from the refrigerator then poured some into a saucepan.

"Do you have any cinnamon sticks?"

He shook his head as he turned on the gas burner. "Afraid not. My cooking is limited to the basics. There's mugs in the cupboard behind you," he added.

Jacqui turned around to open the wooden cabinets. She quickly took down two brown mugs and carried them across to the stove.

Spencer glanced over at her as she stood beside him. It was strange, she thought, that when she was arguing with Spencer she was very sure of herself. But now that they'd made peace of sorts, she wasn't sure of herself or him.

A faint smile touched his thin lips. "I don't think you believe me. About not having women here."

Jacqui fidgeted with the handle on one of the mugs. "Well, maybe I do. Hadley told me you didn't like women."

Spencer threw back his head and laughed out loud. "Is that what he said about me?"

Encouraged by his laughter, Jacqui smiled. "Yes, although I shouldn't have told you. He'll be angry if he finds out I did."

"I doubt that. Hadley and I say anything we want to each other." He turned off the burner, then poured the warm amber liquid into the cups.

"Let's go back to the fire," he suggested, handing Jacqui a mug.

She followed him back into the living room and took a seat on the couch. To her surprise he joined her, leaving a cushion of space between them.

Jacqui carefully sipped her cider and watched the orange flames eat at the oak logs. It was very quiet on Prescott Farms and it seemed to be even quieter here in Spencer's house. The fire crackled and out in the yard the wind whistled through the bare oak trees. Jacqui felt loneliness echoing off the walls, and that bothered her a great deal. She didn't want to think of Spencer being lonely.

"Why did Hadley say you disliked women?" The question came out before she could stop it. Jacqui looked at him, half expecting him to tell her to mind her own business. But he'd probed into her past life today, so she felt it was only fair to be able to question him.

"Probably because I don't do any socializing," he said after a moment.

So he didn't date, she thought. That meant he either wasn't interested in having a woman in his life, or he was still in love with his wife. Either reason disturbed Jacqui.

"Don't you ever want someone to talk to? To share things with?" she asked curiously.

He lowered his cup from his face and turned his head to meet her gaze. His expression was passive. Too passive, Jacqui thought. "I have Hadley, David and Ken, J.T. and you," he added softly.

Jacqui's head shook slowly back and forth. "And that's all you need?"

"Am I supposed to need more? Do you need more?"

Jacqui lifted a hand then let it fall back to her lap. "I like people, Spencer. I like having friends."

He smiled a crooked smile at her. "I do, too. I just don't have women friends."

His words filled Jacqui with all kinds of questions. She longed to ask them, but she figured it might be better to wait before she tried to probe too deeply.

Restlessly she rose from the couch and carried her cider across to the fireplace. The warmth of the fire felt good on her back. She sipped her drink and tried to tell herself that Spencer's personal life had nothing to do with her anyway.

"But now you've come along," he said, his voice filling the quiet room. "And I guess you could call us friends."

Jacqui's warm laughter floated out to him.

"Fighting friends, you might say," she added with an impish smile.

His mouth quirked with a faint grin. "And you're a woman. I suppose that changes things."

Jacqui suddenly found it difficult to swallow. "What things?"

The heel of his palm was rubbing up and down the denim covering his thigh. Jacqui took a deep breath and forced her eyes away from him.

"That I now have a friend who is a woman," he answered.

Smiling, Jacqui looked back at him. It made her happy that he thought of her as a friend. Maybe the fact that he didn't want her to jockey wouldn't always stand between them, she thought hopefully.

"Maybe having a friend who's also a woman won't be too painful for you," she said in a teasing manner.

Spencer doubted that. It had already been painful for him. A sick fear had come over him today on the track as he'd watched her race. If he allowed himself to get closer to Jacqui, he expected that fear would become even worse.

Danielle had made his life a living hell. And even though Jacqui was not like Danielle, he couldn't—or wouldn't—go through another tumultuous relationship. Still Jacqui pulled at his heart no matter how he tried to ignore her.

When Spencer didn't reply, Jacqui went on. "Well, my presence was sort of forced on you. I'm sure Hadley didn't ask your permission before he invited me to live here at Prescott Farms."

"He didn't have to. It was none of my business," Spencer said simply.

Jacqui turned her back to him and placed her empty cup on the fireplace mantel. "I—I wish you didn't think that way, Spencer. This is your home, too."

She didn't hear him cross the room. The touch of his hand on her shoulder caused her to flinch with surprise.

"I'm glad you came, Jacqui. You've changed the place," he said quietly.

Surprised by his words, she looked at him over her shoulder. "Did it need changing?"

His fingers moved gently against Jacqui's shoulders, making a strange feeling curl in the pit of her stomach.

He smiled and Jacqui saw a teasing glint in his eyes. "It was too quiet. Now I have someone to shout at."

Jacqui chuckled softly. "We've done a pretty good job of shouting at each other."

"To be honest, I thought you were going to be an irresponsible little wildcat who played at being a jockey."

Jacqui's eyes searched his and suddenly all she could think of was his closeness, the curve of his mouth, the warmth in his brown eyes. "And now you don't?"

He grinned sexily and for a moment Jacqui's breath vanished.

"I don't kiss little wildcats."

"And you don't like women," she whispered the reminder.

"I like you, Jacqui."

"Spencer—"

Before she could say more, he turned her around to face him. Jacqui felt herself melting as his hand curved against her cheek. Resisting was not in her thoughts as his head bent down to hers.

Slowly, tauntingly, his lips brushed back and forth against Jacqui's. She shuddered at the erotic touch and her hands reached out and held on to each side of his waist.

"It frightened the hell out of me to watch you ride today," he murmured against her cheek.

Jacqui was struck by the intensity of his words. She wondered why he was saying them. She wondered why he was holding her.

"I'm sorry it did, Spencer. You shouldn't feel that—"

"Where you're concerned I shouldn't feel anything," he interrupted. His hands slid to her waist, pulling her closer against him. "But I do, Jacqui. I do."

Jacqui's heart beat sharply in her breast. "In other words, you like me, but you're trying not to."

"Something like that," he murmured, his jaw rubbing sensuously against the side of her neck.

Everything inside Jacqui wanted her to curl her arms around his neck, to give in to the heady feeling his touch produced. But a tiny part of her knew if she did, it would be like yielding to something that could only cause her pain.

It was an effort for Jacqui to flatten both palms against his chest and push herself away from him.

Spencer caught her by the shoulders, preventing her from pulling completely away from him. "Now you're mad at me," he said, using his thumb to push up her chin.

Jacqui met his brown eyes and felt her heart lurch with a brand-new feeling. Spencer was not like any man she'd known in the past. "No, I'm not mad at you," she said breathlessly.

"Then you don't like being here, like this. Being this close to me."

His husky, masculine voice affected her just as much as his touch. Her legs felt weak. Instead of pushing him away, her fingers curled on his chest. "Yes, I—I do like it," she finally managed to say. "But I— It can't be wise."

"Why?"

Her gaze drifted to his mouth. More than anything she longed to lean forward and kiss him. Instead she slowly shook her head. "We don't get along."

The statement sounded foolish after the kiss they'd just shared. Still she felt compelled to say it, because up until now it was the truth.

"I'm getting along just fine like this," he said, his voice low and intimate.

She let out a long, shaky breath. "You don't like the kind of woman I am, Spencer. I don't like the kind of man you are. I'm independent and you're . . . domineering."

He grinned at her. "So that means we shouldn't be kissing?"

Jacqui blushed at his question. "Kissing tends to lead to other things."

"Jacqui," he said wryly, "I'm not trying to take you to bed."

She blushed again, knowing he was probably seeing her as very young and naive. Yet there was no way she could really explain herself without letting him know how attracted she was to him. And that would be a drastic mistake. Long ago, Jacqui had gotten the impression that Spencer would be the last man to want to entangle himself emotionally with a woman.

"I—I know that, Spencer. It's just that I don't go around kissing men just for the heck of it."

His hands tugged on her shoulders, forcing Jacqui to lean into him. "I'm glad to hear that, Jacqui."

Jacqui felt lost to him as his fingers tangled in her long hair. He touched her with a gentleness that was so opposite from the forceful man she knew him to be, and that did strange things to her heart.

"I don't want to think of you kissing any man but me," he said.

"And why should I kiss you?" she murmured the question.

"Because I want you to."

For a second time Jacqui could not resist him. His hand slid under her hair and cupped the nape of her neck, drawing her face up to his.

Jacqui closed her eyes and met the touch of his lips. He kissed her hungrily and in spite of her misgivings she kissed him back with equal fervor.

Spencer felt her soft warm body yield to his. The need to make love to her was a fierce thing inside him. He wanted to be part of her. He wanted to love her and know that she was loving him in return. He'd vowed to never need that from a woman, but here he was anyway, needing her with all his heart.

Feverishly his tongue slipped inside her mouth and his hands cupped her bottom, drawing her hips up against his in an age-old gesture of need.

Jacqui moaned as she felt him lowering her to the Indian rug beneath their feet. She was hardly aware of the hard floor against her back. Spencer's fingers fumbled with the buttons of her shirt and then he was pushing aside the lacy scrap of material covering her breast.

The heat from the fireplace spread across Jacqui's face and bared breast. She watched the firelight play over Spencer's sandy-colored hair, saw it flicker in his eyes as he looked down at her. There was a tender quality to his rough features, a softness to his mouth that tugged at Jacqui's emotions.

"You're so beautiful, Jacqui. You can't imagine how much I want you."

Jacqui knew she should be protesting, but couldn't find it in her to do so. He was just as beautiful to her, and she almost wept with longing when his head lowered and his mouth covered a small pink nipple.

Her arms went around his neck, drawing him closer. Jacqui felt an urgent need in him and knew it echoed the same thing she was feeling. There had never been a man she'd wanted or needed this deeply. She wanted to give Spencer every part of her body. She wanted him to love her in every way a man could love a woman.

Spencer heard her gasp as his hands caressed the length of her thighs. He'd never wanted any woman as he did Jacqui at this moment. The room spun dizzily around his head. He buried his face between her breasts and clutched her to him.

"Jacqui. Jacqui," he moaned.

Before she could collect her scattered senses, she felt his fingers on the button of her jeans. It popped free without effort and the zipper glided apart as he pulled it slowly downward.

In that instant Jacqui knew there would never be any man she wanted to make love to other than Spencer. But she couldn't allow it to happen like this. He wanted her. But he didn't love her. That changed everything for Jacqui.

"Spencer, I—I can't do this," she said brokenly.

Somewhere through the grip of his desire, Spencer heard her plea. Taking a deep breath, he rubbed his hands over his face, then gently levered himself away from her.

Jacqui whispered in anguish. "I'm sorry, Spencer, I—"

Spencer glanced over his shoulder to see her pulling her shirt across her breasts. She looked so small and vulnerable to him. Until now there wasn't anything in his life that he held precious. But as he looked at Jacqui, he knew that she had changed all that. She had become very precious to him.

He reached out and touched her hand. "Jacqui, I didn't mean...for things to get so out of hand."

She pushed her hands in her hair and looked at him. There was an expression of regret on his face that made Jacqui wonder if he'd regretted ever wanting to make love to her in the first place.

"I don't usually—" she stopped and started again, feeling the need to explain herself to him. "I couldn't make love to you without my emotions becoming involved. I—I'm just that kind of woman. And, well, we both know that's not the kind of woman you want."

Spencer studied her for long moments while he waited for his breathing to return to normal and the heat inside him to bank down to a slow burn.

As his eyes took in her tangled hair, red-kissed lips, he thought that he could tell her he didn't want just a woman. He wanted her. That she was the only one who could make him feel this way. But the words stuck in his throat.

He'd learned long ago that letting a woman know you needed her was like putting a powerful weapon in her hand.

"And what kind of woman do you think I want, Jacqui?" he asked, his voice husky from the raw need of wanting her.

She shook back the rich, red curls from her face and met his gaze head-on. Her green eyes seemed translucent. Spencer realized he was mesmerized by her warm, sensual beauty.

"The kind who will give you her body, but not her heart," she said softly.

Jacqui's words stabbed him for they made him realize how detached he'd grown from love and even from life. Before Danielle, he'd been a caring, sensitive man. Somewhere along the way he'd hardened. And he hated the idea that Jacqui saw him as that kind of man.

"You think I wouldn't want your heart, Jacqui?"

His hand slid up her arm and curved over her slender shoulder. She was lying only inches away from him. He struggled with the urge to pull her back into his arms.

Totally confused, Jacqui's eyes dropped to the rug beneath them. "I—I don't know," she answered. "You've only just said you wanted to be my friend. Being a friend isn't like being a lover."

"No. It isn't." Impatient with himself and with her, he rolled to his feet and walked a few steps away.

Jacqui studied his broad back. Things were happening between them too quickly. But then Jacqui had to tell herself that wasn't quite true. From the first moment she'd seen Spencer, things had happened to her heart.

"Are you angry at me?" she asked suddenly.

He turned swiftly to face her, confusion marking his face. "Is that what you think?"

"I—I don't know what to think, Spencer."

He grimaced and thrust his hands into the pockets of his jeans. "I'm angry at myself," he said with a heavy sigh. "Let's just leave it at that."

Jacqui refastened her clothing and slowly got to her feet. She'd never felt more confused or torn in her life. She wanted Spencer, probably even more than he wanted her. It was on the tip of her tongue to tell him she wanted to stay here with him tonight, but the logical part of her fought against the idea. She didn't want to be just a night of sex to Spencer. She wanted more, much more from him than that.

"I think I'd better go," she said.

"I guess—" He stopped, a grimace tightening his features. "Yeah, maybe you'd better," he finished.

Jacqui felt cold and empty as she walked toward the door. She tried not to think of how warm and wonderful it had been to be in his arms. "Thank you for the cider. I'll see you in the morning," she said as her hand reached for the doorknob.

"Wait a minute," he said.

She turned a questioning look on him.

He said, "It's freezing. You'll need a jacket."

"It's only a short distance back to the house," she protested, but already Spencer had left the room.

He quickly returned with a heavily lined denim jacket. "The wind is sharp tonight. There's no use in asking for pneumonia," he reasoned.

Jacqui stood motionless as he draped the jacket around her shoulders. It was too big for her. She clutched the front of it together as Spencer's hand lingered on her shoulder.

"I don't really want you to go, Jacqui."

The words were far sweeter than anything she'd ever expected from Spencer. They thrust deep into her heart and pulled her eyes up to his. "I don't really want to go," she whispered to him. "But...I have to."

Spencer knew she was right. Still he dreaded to see her walk out the door. She'd filled the house with warmth and life. She'd filled him with feelings that he'd thought long dead and put to rest. Like a starving man, he wanted to hold on to all that.

"Jacqui, I'm not really the man you think I am."

Jacqui was suddenly trembling inside. "I'm not sure you want me to really know you."

He reached out and brushed the hair back from her forehead. "You could be wrong about that."

Jacqui gripped the jacket edges, fearing that if she didn't grab something, she would reach out for him and then it would be too late to reason out what was happening between them.

Rising on tiptoes, she kissed his cheek. "Good night, Spencer," she said softly, then quickly slipped out the door.

Spencer watched the door click shut behind her. After her footsteps died on the wind, he walked over to the fireplace and stared down into the flames.

Absently his fingers reached up and touched the spot where she'd kissed him. Spencer had never been kissed on the cheek before. He never knew that such a simple kiss could feel so sweet, so intimate.

But then he'd never known a woman like Jacqui, either.

Chapter Six

The next morning Jacqui was up early even though she'd spent a restless night thinking about Spencer and everything that had happened between them. After dressing in a pair of wheat-colored jeans and a teal-green sweater, she tied her loose hair back with a matching printed scarf, then headed to the kitchen. The appetizing smell of breakfast was filtering through the house and Jacqui knew Gertrude would already have an assortment of food prepared.

Even though it was Sunday the housekeeper came to work anyway. Jacqui suspected since Gertrude had no family of her own, she'd rather spend her time here on the ranch with her friends.

"Good morning, Gertrude," Jacqui spoke as she walked into the warm kitchen.

The older woman looked up from her task at the

sink and gave Jacqui a warm smile. "Good morning. Have a nice rest last night?"

Jacqui made a slight grimace. "Not really. I tossed for hours."

Gertrude clucked her tongue. "Not feeling sick, are you?"

Jacqui shook her head as she went to help herself to a cup of hot coffee. "No. Just feeling restless, I suppose. I'll be fine once I get some of your good cooking in me."

Gertrude handed her a plate piled with warm blueberry muffins. "Try some of these."

Jacqui groaned. "Gertrude why do you tempt me like you do? You know these are my favorites. If you keep giving me all these good things to eat I won't make the jockey weight."

The old woman snorted as she went to work scrubbing a dirty saucepan. "A big puff of this Oklahoma wind could blow you away, Jacqui girl."

Jacqui laughed as she sat down at the table with the muffins and coffee. "Me, and about a pound of these muffins along with me."

"Hadley said you made a show of yourself at the races yesterday."

Jacqui smiled as she smeared a muffin with butter. "I think I surprised everyone. Even Palmer Kirkland."

Gertrude placed the clean pot on the dish drainer. "And what about Spencer?"

Jacqui's brows pulled together. "What about Spencer?"

Gertrude made an impatient sound. "You know what I mean. I know that you and Spencer don't gee and haw about you racing."

Jacqui shrugged. "No, it's no secret that Spencer doesn't like me racing," she agreed in a glum voice.

"Tell me something I don't know, girl. Like what he did over at the track?"

Jacqui reached for her coffee. "What he did?" she repeated. "He didn't do anything. What did you think he would do?"

Gertrude wiped her hands on her apron, pulled out a chair, then sat down. "Knowing Spencer, just about anything," she said to Jacqui. "It wouldn't have surprised me if he'd gone out on the track and pulled you off the horse."

Jacqui shook her head and bit into her muffin. Once she'd swallowed, she said, "Gertrude, that's rather melodramatic, don't you think?"

The housekeeper folded her arms across her breasts and leaned back. "Spencer isn't like most men. When he feels strongly about something he sets his mind like a balky mule."

That was the same impression Jacqui had of him. It was one reason why she knew it would be fruitless to dream of any kind of serious relationship with Spencer. He would never accept her racing. It would stand between them like a cold, brick wall.

"I'm pretty stubborn myself, Gertrude. He would've had his hands full if he'd tried to prevent me from riding. But actually Spencer was ... nice to me. After the races he invited me up to his house for a cup of cider."

Gertrude's blue eyes widened. "He what?"

"After the races he—"

"Yes, I heard that, but did you go?"

Jacqui laughed at the older woman's stunned expression. "Yes, I did."

"Land sakes! Hadley won't believe this. There hasn't been a woman in that house, not even me to do the cleaning!"

It was Jacqui's turn to look shocked. She hadn't taken it so literally when he'd said that. But he'd invited her. What did that mean?

Afraid to read too much into it, Jacqui waved her hand and forced her voice to be light. "It's been a long time since his wife died," she said, placing her half-eaten muffin back on her plate. "His outlook on things has probably changed."

"Maybe so," Gertrude mused aloud. "Funny thing, though, I didn't notice any change in him till you came along."

Jacqui felt a blush burning her cheeks. She was definitely glad Gertrude couldn't see into her head as it replayed the moments she'd spent in Spencer's arms.

"It's not what you're thinking," Jacqui firmly told her. "It's just that I bullied Spencer into accepting my presence here on the ranch. And since we work together throughout the day, he and I both decided it would be much better to be friends."

Gertrude shook her head in a disbelieving way and rose. "You just don't get it, honey," she told Jacqui as she went to pour herself a cup of coffee. "Spencer doesn't like women. Period."

"I know that. But he likes me."

"You think so?"

"That's what he told me."

Gertrude was silent for a moment as she looked down into the cup she was holding. "Spencer's like a son to me, Jacqui. I love the guy, even though there are things about him that make me want to pinch off his head. But—"

Jacqui turned her head to look at Gertrude. "But what?" she asked.

"Spencer's mother deserted him and his father, you know. And then there was Danielle. Both women hurt him deeply. They warped Spence, you might say. And I just don't want you getting the idea that he..."

When the housekeeper failed to go on, Jacqui made an impatient gesture. "He what?" she urged.

Gertrude let out a long breath. "That he might care for you, Jacqui. Because I think Spencer is beyond loving a woman now. He might use one, but he'd never love one. I don't want him to use you. You're too precious for that, honey."

Jacqui felt herself shiver. "You make him sound so...so heartless," she said.

Gertrude shrugged. "It's not that he's heartless, actually. It's more like he's forgotten he has a heart."

The kitchen was warm and cozy, but Jacqui suddenly felt cold. "Was his marriage that bad?"

"Bad is not the word, Jacqui. Danielle was hell on wheels and should have never married anyone, especially not a man like Spence. He wanted a wife and family. Danielle couldn't, or wouldn't, give him either one. She was an independent rebel right down to the last moment of her life."

"Why do you say that? What happened?" Jacqui asked. That Spencer had been hurt and disillusioned by the woman he loved was an unbearable thought.

"That's not something for me to tell you, Jacqui. You'll have to ask Spencer about it yourself. All I'll say is that he was crushed by the accident and what led up to it."

Jacqui couldn't imagine what had actually occurred, yet she could tell from Gertrude's attitude that it had been something terrible. What had Spencer gone through? she wondered. Would he ever be close enough to her to tell her?

Swallowing to ease the tightness in her throat, Jacqui's eyes met Gertrude's solemn expression. "So you think I'd be crazy to think I'm the one woman who could make it all right for him again?"

Gertrude nodded. "I think you'd be asking for one big heartache, Jacqui girl."

Jacqui turned back to her breakfast, even though most of her appetite was gone now. She'd spent the bigger part of the night telling herself exactly what Gertrude had just pointed out. Getting involved with Spencer would be asking for heartache. But what good was knowing that now? It was already too late for her heart.

The morning was sunny and bright, but the wind was still cool and brisk. Jacqui donned a heavy jacket and walked down to the stables.

Horses loved company, especially horses that were stabled and kept separated from the rest. Three dogs and four goats were allowed to roam the barnyard to supply the horses with companionship. By nature, horses that were bred to run were high-strung creatures, so Spencer made sure that radios were in all the barns, softly playing music to soothe and content the animals.

The music was the first sound that met Jacqui as she entered the dimly lit barn. The smell of prairie hay and fresh wood shavings tickled her nose, eager whinnies called out to her from the horses who'd spotted her.

Jacqui had become very attached to all the horses. As she walked past each stall, she called them by name and gave them a special pat on the nose or a scratch between the ears.

At this time the yearlings were the main focus on the farm. Whatever month a foal was born, it automatically became a two-year-old the January of their second year, and two-year-olds were the ones who ran in the futurities for big stakes.

Jacqui had learned that since Oklahoma's weather was usually mild, racing at Blue Ribbon Downs began in February and lasted all the way through November. A hundred and sixty-five days of racing compared to seventy at Ruidoso, New Mexico.

There were already trial heats for futurities and derbys and Spencer was presently breaking several colts and fillies due to run late in the summer, including Bold Tyrant.

The black colt had become one of Jacqui's favorites almost from the first day she'd seen him. In the past weeks she'd watched him grow even heavier and stronger as he matured into a beautiful stallion. Yet despite his growth, he was still a colt at heart with the insatiable need for love and affection. Each time he saw Jacqui he pawed and pranced and strained to poke his nose through the boards of his stall door.

As Jacqui approached this morning, he called out to her with a shrill, stallion's call. Jacqui laughed and climbed up on the door so that she could reach over and stroke his shiny black neck.

"You beautiful darling, did you think I was going to ignore you this morning?"

The colt answered by nuzzling Jacqui's shoulder. She smiled, enjoying his fondness for her.

"You're such a handsome boy, Bold Tyrant. Once the mares around here get a look at you, you'll have them all acting like shameless hussies," she said, then leaned over and planted a kiss on his nose.

His black head bobbed up and down as though he understood every word Jacqui had said. She laughed out loud and continued to rub him behind the ears.

"You're spoiling the hell out of that horse."

Jacqui's head jerked around at the sound of Spencer's voice. She hadn't heard him enter the barn and she wondered how long he'd been watching her.

"I'm only giving him a little attention," she said a bit defensively. "Besides, he's still a baby," she reasoned.

"Baby," he repeated mocking. "That 'baby' as you call him is now old enough to use for breeding."

Jacqui turned her back on the horse and, sitting on the stall door, she found herself almost at eye level with Spencer.

There was a cool look on his face, and Jacqui thought how different he appeared from the man she was with last night. She'd believed that the time they'd spent together had changed things between them. She'd hoped this morning that he would greet her with a smile or gentle word. Last night in his quiet house,

Jacqui had felt so close to him. Hadn't he shared in any of that closeness? she wondered dismally.

"He's still a colt at heart," she said. "It's good for him to know he's loved."

Spencer's lips thinned to a mocking line. "And what's he going to do when he's out on the track and in the gates? Expect the jockey to kiss him instead of spank him across the finish line?"

Jacqui scowled at his sarcasm. "There's a time for kissing and a time for spanking," she said. "You want him to run for you. But why should he, if he doesn't receive love in return?"

He eyed her through narrowed lids and Jacqui felt a spark of desire even though he irritated her with his hard-nosed ideas.

This morning he was wearing a gray Stetson that was obviously an old one. There were sweat stains around the band and the front of the brim had softened from the repetitive tug of his fingers. It dipped crookedly in the center, giving his face a rakish look. A brown jacket covered his broad shoulders. Flecks of hay clung to the fabric, telling Jacqui he'd already been hard at work.

"Too much love will make him soft," he said with a confidence that rankled Jacqui.

Bold Tyrant nudged his nose between Jacqui's arm and her side, and she automatically reached to stroke him.

"That's just your opinion," Jacqui told him, thinking that was probably the way he viewed relationships between men and women—that a man who allowed himself to love a woman was in danger of letting himself become soft and vulnerable.

"Spoiled horses are rarely good runners," he said, his eyes glancing away from her.

Jacqui jumped down, landing only a step or two from Spencer. Her green eyes sparked at him. "Spoiling and loving are entirely two different things," she pointed out.

Spencer looked back at her and felt all his senses stand at attention. Besides being beautiful, there was a strange mixture of fire and innocence about Jacqui. He wanted to protect her and make passionate love to her at the same time.

Last night when she'd left him, a part of Spencer had known it was the only sensible choice for both of them. But the bigger part of him had felt very empty and rejected. It had been years since he'd touched a woman, years since he'd even wanted to. It had been even longer since he'd opened the door on his feelings as he had to Jacqui. She'd shut it, before ever bothering to take a look, and that had hurt him most of all.

"I suppose you think he'd run his best for you?" he said, his mouth suddenly curling with dry amusement.

Jacqui's chin tilted upward in defense. "I know he would. He'd give me his best without me even having to ask for it."

Spencer made a disbelieving grunt. "That's a rather brash statement, young lady."

Jacqui shook her head. "Not brash. Just sure. If you'd let me ride him, I'd prove it to you."

His face was suddenly stiff and impersonal. "You'll not be riding Bold Tyrant under any circumstances."

"You're a stubborn man, Spencer Matlock. I thought you liked to win," she said quietly.

"I live to win," he said brusquely, then gently pushed her aside. "And if you really want to help, you can go get Miss Moon Shadow and the gray mare next to her and bring them out to the walker."

Jacqui didn't waste time arguing. She hoped that if they could get closer, and he really got to know her, he would trust her with his horses. Yet sadly she doubted he'd ever trust her with his heart. And that was the very thing she longed for the most.

Spencer was hitching a lead rope to Bold Tyrant's red halter when Jacqui appeared with the other two horses. They attached the animals to the walker, and once Jacqui was out of the way, Spencer flipped a switch, turning on the machine.

Jacqui stood to one side and watched the horses exercising. After a moment Spencer joined her, standing quietly at her side as he mentally noted the animals' conditions.

Bold Tyrant was feeling frisky and playful at being let out of the confining stall. He bucked, pranced and reared, making Jacqui chuckle at his antics.

"Bold Tyrant is feeling good this morning," Jacqui commented.

"Yes, he is."

Jacqui gave him a sidelong glance. He looked so distant that her heart ached. "Are you angry at me, Spencer? Last night I—"

"Last night would be better forgotten," he said coolly.

Jacqui gasped with disbelief. "Forgotten! Spencer, I thought you said you'd like for us to be friends! And I said I'd like that, too. What are you saying now?

That you want to take it all back? That you've discovered you don't really like me, after all?''

She stepped closer to him. Out of sheer frustration her small hands reached for his chest and grabbed up fistfulls of his jacket. "You really are a swine, Spencer!''

"Damn it, Jacqui, that's not what I mean!" he grated out, a rueful look taking hold of his features.

Jacqui let out a heavy breath. "Then what should we forget? That we kissed? That you wanted to make love to me?''

He didn't answer and the agony she saw in his face left a squeezing path between her breasts. Her fingers relaxed their hold on his jacket and flattened against his chest.

"Spencer, last night I wanted you to make love to me," she confessed. "Is that what you want me to forget?''

Closing his eyes, he shook his head. "I was awake all night, Jacqui," he murmured. "I kept thinking how it was to kiss you. To hold you. What it would be like to make love to you. I couldn't get any of that out of my mind. But when I tried to imagine what it would be like afterward, I couldn't. I was afraid. I was afraid to imagine you and me together for any length of time."

Tears burned the back of Jacqui's eyes and she suddenly wanted to hold him close, to assure him that her love would never hurt him. But he didn't know she loved him, and from what he'd just told her, he wasn't ready to know it.

She was looking at him, trying to decide what to say, when he opened his eyes to look at her regretfully.

"Funny, isn't it, hearing me admit to being afraid? I know that around here I have a reputation for being a tough, hard man. I guess you think I've done a good job of pulling the wool over everyone's eyes."

Jacqui slowly shook her head. "Spencer, having feelings doesn't make you weak. I believe I'm a strong person, but every time I look at you I feel afraid."

Doubt was in his eyes as he clasped both her hands in a protective way. "How could you be afraid of me, Jacqui? I'd never, ever hurt you. My God, my protectiveness of you has caused us more than one argument."

She smiled wanly up at him. "Yes, it has. But that's not what I meant. I'm not afraid of you. Just afraid of what you do to me."

His face relaxed and Jacqui smiled as a gleam appeared in his eyes.

"What do I do to you, Jacqui?" he asked with sly curiosity.

"A lady doesn't tell such things," she said with exaggerated primness.

He smiled at that, and she squeezed his hands and smiled back at him. "Do you have the mares fed in the foaling barn?"

"Are you trying to change the subject?" he asked, one corner of his mouth curved sensuously upward.

"No, I'm trying to invite you to go to church with me. Services start at eleven. If I help you, we can have all the feeding finished before then."

It had been a long time since Spencer had been in a church. He used to go with his father, and the idea of attending with Jacqui brought back memories of a sense of family love and belonging. To think that

Jacqui might want to share those things with him touched him in a place that had lain empty for a long time.

A soft tenderness filled him as he looked at her. "I'd like that, Jacqui. What about Hadley, will he be going?"

Jacqui shook her head. "He left early this morning to join Pete Walters for a day of fishing on the Arkansas River. The way he talked, they'll be gone till dark tonight."

"Well, then, we'd better get to work," he suggested.

"Which other horses were you planning on walking this morning? I'll go get them," Jacqui told him.

Spencer started in the direction of the big barn. "No, I'll get them. You start feeding the mares. You know what to give them, don't you?"

Spencer stopped to look back at her in a questioning way. Jacqui began to patiently list the ingredients, ticking them off on her fingers as she went. "Oats, sweetfeed, bran, vitamin pellets, and hay and water, of course," she added.

He grinned and gave her a wink. "You do know, don't you?"

She made an impish face at him. "Of course I know, Spencer. I know a lot about a lot of things. One of these days you're going to realize that."

Spencer laughed at her words as he continued on toward the barn. Jacqui watched him go, thinking that the sound of Spencer's laughter was the very best sound of all here on Prescott Farms.

* * *

The chores took longer than either one of them had anticipated. Once they were finished, Jacqui hurried to the house and changed quickly into a deep blue dress that buttoned down the front and belted at the waist.

She barely had time to vigorously brush her hair and dab a bit of color on her face before Spencer arrived to pick her up.

Jacqui slid onto the pickup seat, noticing that Spencer was bareheaded and had changed into dark blue jeans, white shirt and olive tweed sports jacket. He looked very nice and Jacqui told him so.

To her surprise the compliment brought a tinge of color to his cheeks, as if he wasn't used to hearing such things.

He absently fingered the black Stetson he'd left lying on the seat between them. "You look very nice yourself, Jacqui," he said simply.

Jacqui laughed as she looked down at her hands now clutching her white Bible. "I only hope Reverend Simpson doesn't look at my hand when he shakes it. He may find horse manure under my fingernails."

Spencer shook his head and chuckled. He'd never known a woman who could work so hard, and then quickly transform herself into the soft, feminine picture that Jacqui now made.

The church Jacqui attended was only a few miles from the ranch. It was a small, clapboard church with a congregation of plain, hardworking people, mostly families who lived in the immediate area.

They were a bit late when Spencer stopped his truck in the graveled parking area out in front. The congregation was on their feet, singing "Onward Christian Soldiers" when Jacqui and Spencer entered and found a space in an empty pew. The pastor, who also acted as the songleader, was standing in front of the pulpit, his arms moving in time with the piano music. He smiled as he spotted Spencer.

"Let us now turn to page 183 in our hymnals," Reverend Simpson instructed once the song ended. "And this time," he added, "I want to hear the rafters rattle."

Spencer picked up a hymnal and opened it to the requested page, then held it so that he and Jacqui could share it.

Jacqui looked up at him and gave him a soft little smile. His eyes caught hers for one special moment, and suddenly, without warning, Jacqui knew that she loved this man standing beside her, that he was the only man she would ever love, the only man she could share her life with. She decided it was a contented feeling to know her own heart, even if Spencer didn't know his.

Later, as they sat on the worn, wooden pew, listening to Reverend Simpson speak of the importance of loving one's family, friends, and fellow man, Jacqui reached over and caught hold of Spencer's hand. He clasped it tightly in his warm fingers, and Jacqui sent up her own prayer.

Chapter Seven

Is Gertrude fixing dinner?" Spencer asked when they were in the pickup headed back to the main highway.

Jacqui crossed her legs and smoothed down the skirt of her dress. "No. I told her not to bother since Uncle Hadley would be out all day."

"Would you like to drive into town and have dinner?"

Jacqui was surprised by his offer. Spencer didn't get off the ranch unless it was a necessity.

"I hadn't thought about it. But that would be nice," she agreed.

At the highway he turned the pickup toward Sallisaw, reached for his hat and jammed it on his head.

"The day is beautiful," Jacqui commented as she looked eagerly out the windshield. "I can't believe the trees are already budding. It stays cold for a long time in Ruidoso. Uncle Claude loved the snow and the cold, though. You couldn't have gotten him away from the mountains for any reason."

Spencer glanced her way. "I guess you still miss him."

A shadow crossed Jacqui's face. "I'll always miss Uncle Claude," she confessed in a quiet voice. "He was a father to me, Spencer."

"Yes, I know that."

A smile suddenly lit her face, transforming it. She looked over at Spencer. "I was ten years old when he put me on my first racehorse. I was frightened to death, but I was even more determined to show him I could ride well."

Spencer's brows pulled together in a disapproving frown. "Ten years old! Was the man crazy?"

Jacqui laughed. "He met everything in life head-on, and he taught me to do the same. I've found down through the years that things are so much easier if you run to meet them instead of run away from them."

His eyes remained on the highway. Just when Jacqui decided he wasn't going to respond, he said, "So Claude is the one who really got you into jockeying."

Jacqui nodded. "He said I had a natural instinct for it. And I believe I do, too. Take Stormin' Home, for example. My instincts kept telling me the horse was not a lead horse."

"And your instincts paid off," he said with a faint frown. "I could have told you the same thing, Jacqui. I've watched that horse run at least ten times and every time he faded in the home stretch. I knew it was the way he'd been ridden."

Jacqui quickly turned sideways so that she was facing him. "Well, darn it, Spencer! Why didn't you tell me that before the races?"

"Several reasons."

"I'd like to hear at least one."

"For one thing you're strong-minded, Jacqui. You probably wouldn't have taken my word for it, anyway."

"That's not true. You're a wonderful trainer, Spencer. I respect your opinion where horses are concerned."

Spencer glanced at her, then looked back to the highway. It was so strange to hear her compliment him. It touched him even more to know that she respected his skill as a racehorse trainer. Danielle had been so quick to ridicule and criticize. She'd never had any faith in him.

"If you really want to know the truth, Jacqui, the main reason I didn't tell you was that I didn't want you to win."

Yesterday those words would have infuriated Jacqui, but today all they did was confuse her. Shaking her head, she said, "That doesn't sound as if you like me. It sounds more like you hate me."

A sheepish look came over his face, an expression that Jacqui had never seen on him before.

"Call me selfish, possessive, domineering or whatever else you want to. I just don't want you racing, and I thought if you got off to a bad start you'd be discouraged from riding again."

Jacqui looked at him and then out the windshield as she tried to make sense of his words. "Spencer, I've been in this business for a long time. I've been riding professionally since I was sixteen, and a bad race is something that happens from time to time to owners, trainers and jockeys alike, you know that. It would take much more than that to discourage me."

"I know. I've already tried several things on you and none of them have worked," he said.

Jacqui had to laugh, she just couldn't help it. "Spencer, you are wicked. You even admit to being wicked."

"If my being wicked will keep you from breaking your neck, then I'll be wicked."

She let out a tense breath and recrossed her legs. "If you would see things logically, Spencer, you would see what a wonderful partnership we could have."

Spencer's eyes slid down her silken clad leg. "What kind of partnership?"

"You know. With the horses. The best trainer and the best jockey. Put us together and we're bound to win," she said with easy confidence.

"Damn it, Jacqui, you're the most persistent little thing I've ever known. How many times do we have to go over this?"

Jacqui didn't answer. There wasn't any point in it. Instead she ignored him and stared out at the scenery.

After a few moments passed Spencer said, "I suppose you're going to ride again for Palmer Kirkland."

Jacqui turned her head to face him. "Yes, and anyone else who wants me to ride. But I wouldn't, not if I could ride for you," she added.

There was something intimate in her voice. It caught at Spencer and forced him to study the lovely, serious lines of her face. "Why? Why would you ride for only me?"

Jacqui felt her cheeks grow warm beneath the intensity of his look. "Because I . . . just would." Because I love you, Spencer, can't you see it, she wanted to tell him. "I admire the way you work and care for horses. I like you. And I'd rather know I was riding to win for you instead of some person who means nothing to me."

Was she trying to tell him that he meant something to her? Spencer wondered. His heart soared, but his mind balked at the idea. It was true when he'd told Jacqui he could not envision them together, not in a married sense. Yet on the other hand, marrying Jacqui, loving Jacqui, was all his heart could see.

"That almost makes me feel good, Jacqui."

Jacqui's eyes widened and she sat straight up in the seat. "Really, Spencer? You mean you agree with me? I can ride just for you?"

Seeing the eager, hopeful look on her face did something to Spencer. For one split second he wanted to give in just to make her happy. But then he remembered all the times he'd given in to Danielle and in the end nothing had made her happy.

"No. And let's not start arguing about this all over again."

Jacqui agreed with him. Where this subject was concerned, all they did was go around in a pointless circle. "You're right," she said, suddenly smiling at him. "I want to enjoy this day and being with you. I don't want us to argue. Let's talk about something else."

He smiled as he felt his mood lift to match hers. "What else do we know to talk about besides horses?" he asked.

By now they'd reached town. Jacqui watched him flip on the turn signal and head down a side street.

"Food," she answered.

"Food?" It was difficult for Spencer to think of food when his mind insisted on running toward more physical thoughts.

"Yes. We are going to eat, aren't we?"

"Yes, we are," he agreed, after pulling to a stop in front of a locally owned restaurant. "Sunday dinner. Together. Maybe I'll stuff you until you go over the one hundred thirty pound limit."

Jacqui laughed. "I only weigh a hundred and ten pounds, Spencer. This is going to have to be a big meal to do that. Besides, you said we weren't going to talk racing."

"You're right," he said, reaching to help her step down from the truck. "So I'll tell you that I enjoyed going to church with you. Thank you for asking me."

She linked her arm through his as they walked to the entrance. "Thank you, Spencer. I enjoyed having you with me."

They had a delicious meal of roast beef and all the trimmings, even fat yeast rolls. Jacqui did stuff herself, but it didn't worry her.

She never had to watch what she ate. During the day she worked hard, and the riding, especially, kept any excess weight off her small frame.

Throughout the meal, both of them kept their word. Horses or racing was never mentioned. On the way home Spencer began to tell Jacqui a bit about the Indian history attached to the area. It fascinated her to think she was living on land that had once been inhabited by five tribes.

She asked him many questions and he informed her he had several books on the subject if she'd like to read them. Jacqui wasn't quite sure if he extended the offer more as an invitation to visit his house, or if he was only thinking of loaning her the books.

Whatever the reason, Jacqui jumped at the offer. She didn't want this time with Spencer to end. He'd been so distant and cold for so long. It was like a soothing balm to her heart to have him smile and talk with her as though he valued her companionship.

As they drove home, Jacqui's thoughts went one step further, asking herself if Spencer would be a man who would also value her love.

Back at the farm, Spencer drove past the main house and stopped the pickup in front of his smaller house. When they entered the living room there were still orange coals glowing in the fireplace. Spencer threw a couple of logs on the dying embers and invited Jacqui to have a seat.

"The books are in the bedroom," he explained. "It won't take but a minute to find them."

Spencer disappeared through a narrow doorway at the end of the room. Jacqui relaxed on the couch and looked around the room once again. This time she realized why there was a starkness to the place. It wasn't the lack of furniture, it was the lack of family-type items.

Although the wall was covered with photos of racing victories, there wasn't a single photograph of a loved one to be seen. Not his wife or mother. Not even of his father, a man whom Jacqui had learned Spencer had virtually adored. She wondered if he kept any photos hidden out of sight so as not to remind him of all he'd lost.

Spencer returned, carrying three hardback books. He crossed the room and sat down on the couch a small distance from Jacqui. "Here they are, I hope you enjoy them," he told her.

She took the books from him and scanned the information on the inner flaps. "I didn't know you read," she said. "It surprises me that you like history."

Grinning faintly, he shrugged. "Jacqui, there's a lot you don't know about me."

She looked up to his face, her heart beating sharply as she encountered his brown eyes. "I'd like to know you, Spencer."

The fire suddenly gave a loud hiss. One of the logs caught flame and sent a shower of sparks out over the hearth. Yet neither Spencer nor Jacqui turned their heads to look.

"Last night you didn't act as if you did," he said.

"That was different," Jacqui reasoned. "That was physical."

"So," he said, suddenly leaning back against the couch and crossing his ankles in a relaxed position. "You don't want to know me physically, is that it?"

Somehow Jacqui knew he wasn't quite as relaxed as he appeared to be. "That's not exactly what I meant."

Spencer pulled off his hat and placed it on the floor at the end of the couch. "Why is it that women aren't satisfied until they can get inside a man's mind? I'll never understand that," he said.

Jacqui pushed her fingers through her tousled hair and gave him a sidelong glance. "I think you're mistaken, Spencer. A woman would rather know what's in a man's heart, rather than his mind."

He made a gesture of disbelief. "Well, that leaves me out. I've been told many times that I don't have a heart."

"Why would anyone say that to you?"

"Why indeed?" he asked wryly. "If I remember correctly you insinuated the same thing."

"I didn't. I called you arrogant and a few other things, but not heartless."

Spencer reached over and caught hold of Jacqui's hand. Slowly he pulled it to his chest until her palm was flattened over the region of his heart.

Jacqui's hand felt the warmth of his chest, the beat of his heart.

"I do have a heart, Jacqui. I just don't think there's anything left inside it."

All at once Jacqui had the greatest urge to cry. She loved this man. Was he trying to tell her that he was too empty inside to love her back? That a woman before her had taken all the love he'd had to give?

"I can't believe that, Spencer. You care about things. I've seen the love and affection you give the horses, the respect and fellowship you have with Hadley. And I think you even care about me, in your own way," she added as she watched his eyes flicker with surprise. "Otherwise you wouldn't care if I broke my neck or not."

He looked away from her, but his hand still covered hers. "When my wife died, I vowed to never get involved with another woman. And since then I haven't even wanted a woman—until you came along."

Jacqui studied his face as conflicting emotions passed over it. It thrilled her to know he wanted her, but wanting wouldn't be enough if his heart wasn't capable of loving.

"Did you love her that much?" Jacqui asked.

He looked back at Jacqui and then, after a few tense moments passed, he shrugged. "I thought...I thought I loved Danielle a lot when I first married her. But later, well, I was just trying to survive in a relationship that was inevitably doomed to end."

"Gertrude hinted that your marriage wasn't a...a happy one. Was it really like that?"

Spencer thrust his free hand into his hair. "Hinted? You mean she didn't tell you?"

Jacqui shook her head. "No. Gertrude thinks you're the son she never had. She respects your privacy."

A wan smile touched Spencer's thin lips. "Gertrude is a truly selfless person. She would have made a wonderful mother. You know, it always seems like those kinds of women—the best kind—are the ones unable to bear children."

"I hope that's not my case. I've always wanted children," Jacqui said.

There was such an odd, pale look on his face that Jacqui asked, "What's the matter? Is something wrong with wanting children?"

"No," he answered a little gruffly. "I always wanted children, too, but as I told you, Danielle didn't. It was just one of many things we disagreed upon. And to answer your earlier question, no, we didn't have a happy marriage.''

Sighing heavily, Spencer rose from the couch and walked across the room. Jacqui watched him as he rested his forearm on the fireplace mantel and stared pensively into the flames.

"It was my fault,'' he said abruptly. "I should have never married her. But when you're twenty years old and believe yourself to be in love, you don't stop to consider many things.''

Jacqui's eyes followed the lean, muscular lines of his body and imagined how he must have looked to young women all those years ago. "Yes, I know what you mean. I didn't stop to consider things about Jay, either. Uncle Claude tried to tell me, to point out things I needed to take another look at. But advising a teenager on their love life is never too successful.''

Spencer looked around and gave Jacqui a brief smile. But then his face grew reminiscent as he said, "Danielle was interested in anything that would get her out of her poor existence. Her folks were the type who didn't care whether they had much or not. And what they did have, Danielle had to share with two sisters and three brothers. She saw marrying me as an escape. I realized that later, but by that time it was too late.''

Jacqui got to her feet and joined him at the fireplace. "Then wasn't she happy? I mean, I'm sure you had so much to offer her.''

He grimaced and dropped his arm from the mantel. "Not the kind of things Danielle wanted. She was never satisfied. She was one of those people who always wanted more. She hated the fact that I trained horses. There wasn't enough money or prestige in it for Danielle. In short, she turned out to be just like my mother.''

Jacqui winced inwardly. She couldn't imagine Spencer being married to such a woman, much less loving her. "What did she want you to do?''

"Move to the city. Any big city. She wanted excitement in her life, and sitting around on a horse farm, watching the grass grow couldn't give it to her.''

Jacqui was beginning to get the whole picture and it wasn't a pleasant one. "I take it you wouldn't move?''

Spencer shook his head. "Jacqui, my father lived here. He was the only family, the only close living relative I had. I didn't want to be hundreds of miles away from him. Besides, training horses was what I loved. I'd given up many things for Danielle but I wasn't going to give that up. It was a constant source of argument between us.''

"Yes, I can see that it would be.'' Just as her riding was always a bone of contention between herself and Spencer, Jacqui thought sadly. "But surely she could see how much you loved your work,'' Jacqui reasoned out loud. "Did she have a job?''

Spencer's smile was bitter. "Danielle couldn't discipline herself to stay with a job. She always had excuses to quit. Like she was overworked, underpaid, or wasn't able to get along with co-workers.'' He sighed and thrust his hands into his jean pockets. "Finally I encouraged her to go to college. I'd hoped with more education, she could have a better job that would suit her and maybe satisfy her in some way that I couldn't.''

Jacqui turned toward the fire and felt its heat wash over her face. She was at least two or three steps away from Spencer, but knowing he was sharing part of himself with her made him feel much closer.

"Did it? I mean, did college make things any better?" Jacqui asked.

Spencer shook his head. There was a cold, detached look on his face that made a knot form in the pit of Jacqui's stomach.

"It was only a matter of weeks before people were coming to me, informing me they'd seen Danielle out with young college men."

Jacqui was stunned. A moment passed before she spoke. "I don't understand, Spencer. Why did you stay with her? Why didn't you get a divorce? Not that I condone divorce, but when two people are unhappy... I—I couldn't stay with Jay after discovering he was unfaithful to me."

Pulling his hands from his pockets, he walked slowly over to the windows facing the front yard.

Outside the sky was sunny and blue, and in the far distance Jacqui could see a portion of the stables and the round pen where the yearlings were broken to ride. It was a beautiful, peaceful view and it amazed Jacqui that Spencer's wife had rebelled against all of it. Yet even more, it was difficult for her to understand how Danielle had rebelled against a man like Spencer.

"I think it was because I'd never had a family to speak of, Jacqui. Since my mother left us when I was very small, it was always just Dad and myself. I wanted a family more than anything. I thought if I hung on, tried hard enough, I could have one with Danielle. I didn't want to be a quitter like my mother had been." He shrugged in a negligible way, but Jac-qui knew the memories were still hurting him.

"But in the end," Spencer went on, "it hadn't mattered. She was killed and everything came to an end."

"Hadley said that she'd been killed not far from here. Had she been coming here to the farm?"

Spencer didn't turn to look at her. Even so, Jacqui could tell from the sound of his voice that there was a bleak look on his face.

"I don't know."

"Oh." She didn't know what else to say. Perhaps there wasn't anything left to say, she thought.

Spencer suddenly turned and looked at Jacqui. "She came home late that evening about dusk. It was a hot summer, and I'd just gotten in from working here on the ranch. She slammed in the house with a furious look on her face. I asked her what was wrong and she said, 'I'm pregnant, that's what wrong! You've gotten me pregnant just so you can keep me chained to this house while you go out and play with your horses! Well, I won't have it! I'm getting an abortion!'"

He stopped and shook his head, wiping a hand across his forehead as if he wished to wipe away the memory. "I roared back at her that she wasn't going to kill my child. Danielle threw an angry fit, then ran out the door yelling that one way or the other she'd get rid of the baby. Before I could stop her, she'd jumped into her car and spun down the road, driving like the devil himself. I jumped in my pickup and followed her, hoping to stop her. I don't really know where she was going, if she was merely running away, or going to see Hadley. He was one of the few friends she had, and he often tried to help her, to soothe over her angers. But we'll never know the answer to where she was headed. Danielle was traveling about eighty when the car suddenly spun out of control and flipped over on its side. It skidded about fifty feet off the highway and into a grove of trees. Danielle was already dead by the time I reached her."

Jacqui tried to speak, then realized her throat was too tight to utter a word. She swallowed, then asked hoarsely, "You saw it happen?"

He nodded. "It was like watching a nightmare, one that I had no control over, or couldn't wake up from." He went on in a flat voice, "I suppose that's the way our whole marriage had been, too. A nightmare that I could do nothing about."

Jacqui shook her head disbelievingly. "I don't know what to say, Spencer. I can't imagine anything that terrible. Your wife and your baby. Do you think she was deliberately trying to kill herself?"

Spencer let out a heavy breath and walked back over to Jacqui and the fire. "Sometimes I've wondered that myself. She was certainly driving as though she wanted to kill herself. But I think that Danielle was too much in love with herself to take her own life. Whatever the case, I felt very guilty about her death, about the baby. I kept thinking if I'd only been a better husband. If I'd tried harder, neither one of them would be dead."

"Oh, Spencer! You should never have thought that!"

He shrugged with resignation. "Yes. Well, it took me a long time to see the truth in that. But I've finally come to realize that no matter what I'd done I couldn't control Danielle's fate."

Jacqui's hands were clasped tightly behind her back as she thought about Spencer and the woman he'd lost. It was a terrible thing to have happen to him and one that he hadn't deserved. But he was still a young man and all of that was behind him now. If he could only see how much Jacqui loved him, respected him as a man, wanted him to be happy.

"I'm so sorry, Spencer. But I'm glad you told me about it."

He suddenly closed the distance between them. Jacqui looked up into his face as his hands settled warmly on both her shoulders.

"I wanted you to know, Jacqui," he murmured. "I wanted you to understand why I can't let you ride my horses."

Jacqui frowned. "I thought you didn't want me to ride because you considered jockeying a man's job."

A sheepish look came over Spencer's face. "That's just— I wanted you to think that. All along I'd been thinking you'd left your husband for the same reasons my mother left, and my wife—" He stopped and shook his head. "I was determined to use something to keep a wedge between us. But now it's not like that."

"I don't understand, then, Spencer. Why are you still against me riding?"

"Because now I care about you, Jacqui. Yesterday when I watched you race, it was like I was seeing

Danielle in that car all over again. I don't want to see you killed like she was killed."

Jacqui let out a small gasp. "But Spencer," she whispered in confusion, "My riding has nothing to do with how Danielle was killed."

His fingers tightened on Jacqui's shoulders, conveying to her just how strong his feelings were. "It does, Jacqui. For a long time I felt responsible for Danielle's death. It was like living in hell, but I finally lifted myself up out of all that. But if you were injured or killed riding one of my horses, I don't think I'd ever get over it."

Tears welled up and burned Jacqui's eyes. In his own way, Spencer was telling her he loved her, Jacqui realized. Yet at the same time she also knew that his loving her wasn't enough. He had to trust, to know that she wouldn't purposely endanger her life as Danielle had.

"Spencer," she said, lifting her hand and touching his cheek. Her eyes searched his, begging him to open his heart to her. "I love you. Maybe now is the wrong time to tell you. But I want you to know how I feel. I want you to see that Danielle was far different from me."

A blank look came over his face, as though the roof had just caved in on both their heads. "You—you love me?" he whispered.

"It can't be that surprising."

Wordlessly he shook his head and pulled her against him. Jacqui pressed her cheek against his chest and wound her arms around his waist, letting her touch tell him exactly what she'd told him with words.

"I haven't been particularly nice to you, Jacqui," he said with much regret.

Jacqui's mouth moved into a faint smile. "There's been times I've wanted to kill you. You've got the perfect patent for making me angry."

A chuckle suddenly rumbled in his chest. "You do a hell of a job stirring me up, too, Jacqui." His hand closed over her chin and lifted her face up to his. "And for whatever it means to you, I love you, too."

Jacqui's eyes shimmered with unshed tears. "It means more to me than anything, Spencer," she said softly.

He groaned and bent his head, finding her lips with his. Jacqui clung to him, hungry for his touch, for his love.

Spencer held her close, showering her face and lips with kisses. His hands meshed in her hair, holding her head tightly as if he feared she was suddenly going to slip away.

"Oh, God, Jacqui," he said after a few moments. "What is this going to do to me? To you?"

She rubbed her soft cheek against his. "It's going to make us happy. If you'll just trust me, you'll see this. I know that right now there's things standing between us. That you—"

Spencer lifted his head, stopping her words. "I don't want to talk about your riding, Jacqui."

An anxious look filled her eyes. "But Spencer, we need to—"

"I don't want to talk about that now. I don't want to think about it now. I just want to hold you like this, Jacqui, and worry about the rest of it tomorrow."

Jacqui silently answered his plea by sliding her arms around his neck and raising her lips to his. For right now, it had to be enough for her to be in his arms and know that he loved her.

Chapter Eight

Early Monday morning Jacqui was down at the stables saddling a mount to take to the track for its galloping exercise.

Nearby, Ken and David were busily cleaning stalls. So far this morning both young men had talked of nothing but Jacqui's races at Blue Ribbon Downs.

"Jacqui, you looked like a streak of lightning on Ima Easy Choice," David said as he shoveled clean shavings into an empty stall.

"And when you came flying up the home stretch on Stormin' Home," Ken added, "I thought Angel Cordero, Jr. had come to town!"

Jacqui chuckled softly. "I'll just bet you did," Jacqui teased. "And since you thought it was Angel riding, you must have bet a lot on Stormin' Home. By the way, you guys haven't told me yet how much you won Saturday."

"Well, er, Jacqui it was like this," David hedged.

Ken, who was leaning against his rake, looked apologetically at Jacqui. "Stormin' Home had been a dud until yesterday. We thought—" He broke off at the disgusted expression on Jacqui's face.

David stuttered, "We—we thought we'd...lose our money if we bet on him."

"It wasn't like we were betting against you," Ken added sheepishly.

"Oh, yeah," Jacqui groaned good-naturedly. "You just compared me to the great Angel Cordero, Jr., but then I find out you didn't even bet on me. You guys really had confidence in me, didn't you?"

"We'll bet on you next time," David promised. "Ken and I will pool our money and—" He suddenly stopped.

Sensing Spencer's presence, Jacqui glanced over her shoulder to see him standing just behind her. Beneath the brim of his black hat there was a tender look on his face for her. Her heart warmed at the sight of him and she gave him a wide smile.

"Good morning," she said softly.

"Good morning," he returned, moving closer and touching her shoulder.

Jacqui was faintly aware that Ken and David were scurrying off to clean another stable, as if they knew that she and Spencer wanted privacy.

"Did you have a good night?" she asked Spencer.

His gloved finger reached out and touched the soft skin beneath her chin. "Yes, I did. And you?"

She nodded, thinking what a drastic change there was in him and between them. It was so good to see the cold look on his face replaced with a warm smile. She hoped it would always be this way. Last night she'd promised him they would be happy. She had to prove that to him today and every day.

"I was just getting ready to take Bound to Win down to the track. How far do you think I should take him?"

"A mile and a half should be fine," he told her, reaching for the cinch on the saddle and testing it. He buckled it a fraction tighter. "It's cold this morning, so keep an eye on him. He might want to buck."

"I will," Jacqui promised. In the past, Spencer's cautions would have rankled her. She'd always thought he was constantly harping safety to her because he thought she was inept at her job. Now she knew that hadn't really been the case. He was actually afraid for her safety. Now that Jacqui understood this, she wanted more than ever to reassure him. "I'll keep a tight rein on him until he's warmed up."

"Here, let me give you a foot up and I'll lead him down to the track for you," he told her.

Jacqui's eyes caught and held his, and suddenly a lump was in her throat. Spencer had never offered to help her mount. In fact he usually stayed completely away when she was working down at the track with the horses. It told her that in a small way, he was reaching out to meet her. And Jacqui loved him for it.

"Thank you, Spencer," she said softly.

For a second there was a look on his face that said he wanted to kiss her. But he must have suddenly remembered Ken and David's presence only a few feet away.

Reaching down, he clasped her leg just above the ankle. With a quick, strong lift from his arm, Jacqui easily swung herself into the saddle and positioned her feet in the iron stirrups. Spencer took hold of the bridle and led her and the horse out from beneath the shed row.

It was a cold, cloudy morning. Jacqui was wearing a thick wool ski sweater in blue and white. As the brisk wind whipped against her, she suddenly thought back to her Uncle Claude and how he'd stayed out on the track, watching the horses work, no matter how cold the weather had been. He would be happy to see Jacqui now. Doing what she loved, with the man she loved.

Spencer kept a taut hold on the horse as he walked them. Beneath her, Bound to Win, impatient at the slow pace, danced sideways and snorted in the cold air. "I thought about you all last night," she admitted shyly.

Spencer glanced up at her and she caught the wry expression on his face. "I thought you said you had a good night?"

Jacqui's smile dimpled her cheeks. "It was. Thinking about you is good."

Spencer's heart surged at her words. "I did a lot of thinking myself, Jacqui. I know you are nothing like Danielle, that the situation between us is entirely different. But—"

They were near the dirt track. Spencer pulled them to a halt and looked up at her. Jacqui gripped the reins as she waited for him to continue.

"I just don't want you to expect too much from me. It's been a long time since— I'm not used to caring for someone," he said, impatient with himself because this wisp of a woman made him feel so uncertain.

With a discerning look, Jacqui leaned down and touched his arm. His free hand reached up and stroked her cheek. "Maybe we should take it a day at a time," he suggested, his voice low.

Jacqui nodded in agreement. She knew Spencer needed time to accept her in his life. In a way, she needed time herself. Even though there was no doubt in her mind that she loved Spencer, she wondered how they could ever cross the chasm between them.

"I think you're right, Spencer," she said softly.

His hand slowly closed over her chin and pulled her face down to him. The kiss they shared was brief, but it was everything Jacqui needed. Because it told her he loved her.

"You'd better get to work," he said after releasing her.

She gave him a little grin then straightened in the saddle. "J.T. is coming off the track now," she told him as she spotted Prescott Farms' other jockey pulling up his mount about fifty yards away from them. "Will you stay and watch me gallop?"

Spencer could see the eager light in her eyes and found he could not refuse her. "Yes, I'll stay and watch," he told her, letting go of Bound to Win's bits.

Jacqui trotted the horse on the track, certain her spirits were as high as the animal she was riding. She could feel the horse's muscles tighten beneath her and knew he would love to get his head down and buck in the cool morning air.

Knowing this, Jacqui kept a tight rein until she felt him warming and loosening. When she did finally let him go, he kicked his heels up a couple of times, but Jacqui had no problem staying in the saddle.

Spencer walked to the cleared area in the center of the track and watched Jacqui and the horse move together. She made a beautiful sight on the animal's back. Her red hair matched the sorrel horse, and streamed away from her back like a bright ribbon in the wind.

In all honesty, Spencer had to admit that she was one of the best jockeys he'd ever seen. And that troubled Spencer more than anything. One part of him wanted to see her ride to glory and to share in her joy of doing it. But the scarred, uncertain side of him wanted to put her far away from the dangers of jockeying. He loved her. But he didn't know what in hell he was going to do about it.

At noon Spencer and Jacqui walked up to the main house to join Hadley for lunch.

The clouds had grown heavier throughout the morning. Now there was a heavy mist that threatened to turn into rain.

Jacqui's sweater was damp by the time they reached the house. She went to her room to change while Spencer joined Hadley in the kitchen. When she came in wearing an aqua-colored shirt, Gertrude was already serving lunch on the table.

"You'd better get in here, girl," she told Jacqui, "before these men eat it all up."

Jacqui laughed and took a seat to the left of Spencer. He gave her a sidelong glance that was meant just for her.

Hadley said, "So, how are the horses this morning, Spence? Has that foal come yet?"

Spencer shook his head while reaching for a cheese sandwich. "No. But it will any time now."

"She's so heavy she looks miserable," Jacqui commented, speaking of the mare.

"I'll check on her several times before the day's over," Spencer said. "If this rain sets in, she'll probably have it tonight. Babies always seem to want to come in a storm."

Gertrude placed steaming bowls of chicken soup in front of everyone and Jacqui reached for her spoon.

"Do you have much spring rain here in this part of Oklahoma?" Jacqui asked.

Hadley was the one to answer. "Usually. Though the last two springs have been dryer than normal. It puts a hell of a cramp on horse trainers. There's not much you can do when it's pouring."

"It rains a lot in Ruidoso in the summer. But it's mostly showers that come and go within an hour or two. It's the—"

The telephone on the kitchen wall suddenly rang, breaking into the conversation.

Gertrude quickly answered it. "Yes, Jacqui Prescott is here. Just one moment, please," the housekeeper spoke into the phone.

At the sound of her name, Jacqui looked up curiously. She didn't get very many phone calls, making her wonder who it could be.

She rose quickly from the table and went to take the phone. "Yes, this is Jacqui Prescott," she answered. "No, I'm sorry. I'm afraid I don't recognize your name," she went on, suddenly feeling both Spencer's and Hadley's eyes boring into her. She looked at the men and shrugged while waiting for the caller to explain himself.

After a moment Jacqui's face brightened and she said eagerly, "Yes, I will be available. Friday, did you say?"

Spencer's eyes narrowed suspiciously and Hadley began to grin.

"Rides," Hadley guessed with the pride of a doting father. "I told you, Spence. It won't be any time at all and Jacqui will have those other jockeys scooting over."

Frowning, Spencer looked away from Jacqui, who was still on the phone, and began to eat his soup. "So you told me before," he muttered.

After a moment Hadley leaned toward the center of the table and said in a low voice, "She loves what she does, Spencer. I'd think twice before I tried to make her choose between it and you."

Spencer's head jerked up at the older man's advice. Pain and anger mixed inside him. "Damn it all, Hadley!" he hissed under his breath. "Don't you think I—"

Spencer broke off suddenly as Jacqui replaced the receiver and returned to the table.

The light of excitement in her heart dimmed as she cast Spencer an uncertain glance. "I'll be riding two mounts Friday," she announced, knowing it wouldn't serve any purpose to delay telling him.

Spencer's face paled, but he said nothing in return.

As Jacqui took her seat she could feel a coldness settling over him. It made her want to weep and throw things at the same time.

"That's wonderful, Jacqui," Hadley spoke proudly. "Who called?"

"Said his name was Bob Barrett. Do you know him?"

Spencer's head jerked around to Jacqui at the same time Hadley's mouth flew open.

"Bob Barrett," Hadley boomed in his deep voice. "Why darlin', he just happens to be one of the most successful trainers around these parts. Next to Spencer, that is," he added tactfully.

"Are you kidding me, Uncle?"

"Not a bit. You're shooting up to big time."

Jacqui gave her uncle a mocking frown. "It's only a couple of allowance races," she explained before he got carried away. "Nothing with a big purse."

"Doesn't matter," Hadley insisted with a broad grin. "You ride for Bob on Friday and the next thing you know you'll be riding in futurity and derby trials."

Hadley was saying everything she'd been wanting to hear. Apparently she was getting a chance to put her foot in the door. Any other time she'd be on her feet doing a happy jig, but Spencer had already squashed her exuberance.

Jacqui picked up her spoon and began to eat her soup. Beside her, Spencer was quietly finishing his lunch. He felt miles away from her, while just a few minutes ago they'd been laughing and enjoying the work they'd shared this morning.

It almost made Jacqui want to tell him she would quit riding racehorses. That she wouldn't ride for anyone else and she wouldn't try to ride for him. That she'd put her whole career aside if it would make him happy. But Jacqui had thought about it long and hard and decided she'd never be happy that way. And in the end, if she wasn't happy, Spencer wouldn't be happy, either.

The problem was Spencer's, not hers. Giving in to him was not the solution. She had to stand up for both the things she loved: him and her riding. She had to make him understand this.

"I'm not going to hold my breath until that happens," she said. "But I am glad about the races Friday."

Hadley began to inquire about the horses she would be riding and Jacqui furnished him with what little information Bob Barrett had given her over the phone.

As they talked, Spencer got up from the table.

"Thanks for the lunch, Gertrude," he told the housekeeper while heading toward the door.

He didn't say a word to Jacqui. Angry at his obvious snub, she opened her mouth to call after him, but he stepped outside before she had the chance.

Hadley saw the perplexed look on Jacqui's face and said, "It appears Spencer's not too keen on you riding for Bob Barrett."

Jacqui threw down her napkin and rose to her feet. "Spencer isn't keen on me riding for anyone," she said.

"And that bothers you?" Hadley asked innocently.

Jacqui raised her brows, she couldn't believe her uncle's question. "Of course it bothers me!"

After Hadley and Gertrude exchanged a pointed look, Jacqui hurried out the door to catch up with Spencer. He was not quite to the barn when Jacqui reached his side. It was raining heavier now and she could feel the water seeping into her shirt and hair.

Spencer glanced over at her briefly. "You should have on a jacket."

She looked down at the blotches of moisture appearing on her shirt. "I wanted to catch up with you. Why did you leave so quickly? You'd barely eaten anything."

"I'd had enough."

"Food or racing talk?" she asked.

"Both."

His long strides brought him to the end of the barn. Jacqui half skipped to keep up with him.

"You're angry, aren't you? You don't want me to ride for Bob Barrett."

Spencer shoved the sliding door open and entered the dim interior of the barn. Jacqui followed him inside, and he slid the door shut behind her.

"I don't want to talk about it," he said, then headed to where feed and hay were stored.

Jacqui stalked after him. "You didn't want to talk about it last night, either!"

Spencer stopped abruptly, causing Jacqui to nearly crash into his back. He reached out and grabbed both her arms, steadying her.

"Because I knew it wouldn't do any good," he said flatly.

"What do you mean by 'good'? For me to say I'll quit riding? Do you think that's what would be good for you? For me?" Jacqui challenged.

Spencer closed his eyes as though he wanted to shut out the sight of her. "You know how I feel, Jacqui. And you know why I feel the way I do. I thought you understood."

Shaking her head, Jacqui reached out and touched his chest. "I do understand, Spencer. But can't you understand my side of things, too? I love to race. It's what I want to do."

"Last night you said I meant more to you than anything. Were you just mouthing words that you thought I wanted to hear?" he demanded.

Jacqui drew in a sharp breath. "How could you ask me that?"

His lean face seemed to harden, making the bones in his cheeks stand out sharply. "It's obvious you care more about jockeying than me. You just accepted two rides."

Her heart sank when she searched his eyes for any sign of yielding and found none. "You couldn't be more wrong," she told him. "And it's totally unfair of you to be doing this to me."

"It's totally unfair of you to put me through the hell of watching you willingly endanger yourself!"

Jacqui made a gesture of helplessness. "The danger isn't that great, Spencer. It's only intensified in your mind because of what happened to Danielle. I shouldn't have to pay because of her misfortune."

A sneer twisted his mouth. "Oh, so now you're a psychologist," he said dryly.

Jacqui couldn't stop the anger from surging up in her like a great, hot wave. She jerked loose from his grasp and backed away. "At least I can see both sides of things. I can see that you love what you do, but I'm not insisting that you give it up! I wouldn't do that to you."

"What I do has nothing to do with us," he barked.

Jacqui couldn't believe his blind remark. "You put
yourself in just as much danger when you climb on
those green yearlings. David told me you've had a
broken arm, a broken collarbone, a crushed ankle—"

"Maybe I'm just not as good a rider as you," he
said with a sarcasm that stung Jacqui. She turned and
slowly walked away from him and out the barn door.

Spencer didn't try to call her back, and Jacqui knew
it was just as well. There was no use arguing, she
thought hopelessly. His mind was closed to her, to
everything.

Jacqui spent the remainder of the afternoon in the
house. The rain prevented any further work with the
horses. It was probably the best, she thought. She
needed time away from the stables and from Spencer.

Any other time she would have been shouting to the
top of the world. A leading trainer had asked her to
ride for him. But Jacqui couldn't find it in herself to
be happy when Spencer was so dead set against it.

For the past hour she'd been sitting in her bedroom, trying to get interested in a novel. So far all
she'd managed to do was stare out the window at the
darkness and the rain spattering against the glass
panes.

She'd never felt so miserable or torn in her life and
she wished that Claude were alive. He would have
known exactly what to say to her to make her feel better.

Jacqui faced the fact that she could never talk to
Claude again. But of course, there was Hadley. He
was always ready to listen to Jacqui and advise her.

Hadley was kind and he loved her. She was thankful that she had him now, if no one else.

Sighing, she rose from the stuffed armchair beside her bed and walked over to the window, wrapping her arms around her waist. Even if Claude was alive, Jacqui doubted he could have helped her now. She'd fallen in love with Spencer, and there could be no turning back for her.

A knock at her bedroom door intruded into her thoughts and pulled her attention away from the window.

"Yes. Come in," she called.

Hadley opened the door and stuck his head in. "Spencer just called up from the barn. The new foal was born a few minutes ago. A filly. She's sorrel with four white anklets."

Jacqui mustered a smile. "That's good."

Hadley scowled with disbelief. "That's all? That's good? Jacqui, get your coat on so we can go down and see her."

Jacqui shook her head. "You go on. I—I'll wait till morning to see her."

Hadley stepped into the room. "I know you've been in here brooding," he told Jacqui, "and I'm gonna tell you right now it won't do any good."

Jacqui raised her brows at her uncle's stern expression. "I haven't been brooding," she insisted. "Just thinking."

"About Spencer, I know."

"I don't want to go down to the barn with him there."

Frowning, Hadley shook his head. "That's ridiculous. You both live here on the farm. You can't avoid him."

Jacqui's head dropped. "I don't plan to. I just don't want to see him tonight," she murmured, her voice trembling.

Hadley went to her and put an arm around her shoulders. "Jacqui, you're like a daughter to me. And if I were your real father I'd still tell you the same thing. If you really care about Spencer, you can't back down and avoid him. You've got to fight for him. He's a hard man in a lot of ways. But he needs you, Jacqui. He's been so alone for a long time."

Jacqui's throat ached with tears. "He wants me to give up riding, Uncle Hadley. He's trying to force me to choose between him and it."

Hadley patted her shoulder. "He only think that's what he wants. It's up to you to make him see differently. And you can't do that in here in your room. So get your coat, honey, and we'll go see that pretty little girl."

Deciding it would be pointless to argue, Jacqui went to the closet and pulled down a rust-colored corduroy coat. While buttoning it, she looked at her uncle. "Do you think I'm selfish? To want both Spencer and my riding?"

He rubbed a hand thoughtfully across his jaw. "I'd think something was wrong with you if you didn't want both."

She smiled faintly. "I guess I'm putting you on the spot, aren't I? You love Spencer as a son. I know you can't take sides between him or me."

Hadley took her arm and guided her out the bedroom door. "I love you both," he said. "I know what Spencer's been through and how he feels. He's afraid of losing you. But I also know how you feel. So as I see it, this is something, darlin', that you'll have to work out yourselves."

Jacqui put her arm through his. "You're being very diplomatic, Uncle Hadley."

He chuckled. "Not diplomatic, honey. Just sensible. Remember, I live here, too."

Jacqui gave him a smile because she knew it bothered him to see her upset, and he was trying his best to lift her spirits. "Yes, I do remember. And thank you for coming to get me. I did really want to see the filly."

He patted her hand with an understanding that came with living sixty-odd years of life. "I know, Jacqui."

It was still raining when Hadley and Jacqui stepped out into the night. They walked quickly to the foaling barn and found the new mother and baby at a stall on the end.

Jacqui saw that Spencer was in another part of the barn, washing his hands and arms beneath a spigot. He dried them and rolled down the sleeves of his denim shirt.

"Pretty one, isn't she, honey?" Hadley asked, making Jacqui turn her attention away from Spencer and back to the stall.

Jacqui nodded, feeling Spencer's presence as he joined them. She didn't turn her head to look at him. Instead she kept her eyes on the mare and her still wet baby.

"You can tell she's got racing blood in her veins. Look at those long, pretty legs," Jacqui commented.

"Nice little pair of hips on her, too," Hadley added.

"You say that about all women," Jacqui teased, making her uncle chuckle.

Hadley glanced at Spencer. "How did the mare do?"

"Fine," Spencer told him. "It was an easy birth."

The sound of his voice pulled at Jacqui. She twisted her head slightly and her eyes clashed with his. He walked closer and leaned his shoulder against the stall.

Neither one of them spoke, yet Jacqui could read what was on his face. The anger was gone, but in its place was bitter disappointment.

As Jacqui stared at him she was certain her heart cracked with every beat it took. The pain of it forced her to finally look away from him and back to the new filly.

"Has she tried to stand yet?" Hadley asked.

"Not yet," Spencer answered. "But I expect she will anytime now."

As if on cue the tiny red filly struggled to gather her long gangly legs beneath her. She made it as far as her front knees then toppled over. The mare got to her feet as if to demonstrate and encourage her new offspring in the proper way to stand upright on all fours.

"Get up little gal," Hadley spoke to the baby. "Your mammy has some warm milk waiting for you."

The three of them watched as the baby tried it again. This time she stood, although her fragile little legs shook.

Emotion thickened Jacqui's throat as she watched the little filly struggle and brace herself for the new life that had suddenly been thrust upon her. She was so weak, so totally dependent on her mother. But Jacqui knew that Spencer would watch over the newborn as he would a child. She would have the best of care, as did all the horses here on Prescott Farms. It was one of the things that made her love him.

The mare began to lick the baby with vigorous swipes, causing the filly to totter precariously.

Hadley chuckled as Jacqui exclaimed, "She's going to knock her over!"

"If she does, she'll get up again," Hadley spoke easily.

It was only a matter of moments before the filly began searching for a taste of her mother's milk. When it finally found the mare's bag and latched hungrily onto a warm teat, Jacqui felt her own maternal instincts stir at the sight.

"They should be fine now," Spencer spoke up. "So I think I'll go on to the house."

Jacqui knew that Spencer was leaving because of her, and pain sliced through her.

"I'm going back to the house, too. What about you, Jacqui?" Hadley asked.

"In a few minutes. I want to look at the baby a bit longer."

Hadley patted her shoulder. "You look her over real good, darlin', 'cause I want you to pick out a few names for her."

Jacqui smiled at her uncle. "I will," she promised.

Hadley left the barn then, and Jacqui turned her attention back to the mare and the foal. She felt

Spencer move away, and sadness filled her. This morning he'd kissed her. They'd smiled and touched and talked like lovers. Jacqui couldn't understand how he could be such a cold stranger now.

"It won't do you any good, you know."

Thinking he'd already left the barn, Jacqui was startled by the sound of Spencer's words. Her head jerked around to see him standing a few feet behind her.

"What are you talking about?"

"Naming the baby. The AQHA will name it whatever they see fit, no matter how many names you send in."

He was talking about the American Quarter Horse Association, where the baby's birthday, name, color and family tree would be registered.

"Not always," Jacqui told him. "Uncle Claude and I had a few names accepted for our horses. It never hurts to try."

To her amazement one corner of his mouth lifted in a wry smile. "Always the persistent little Jacqui, aren't you?"

She jammed her hands into the pockets of her coat. "I'm not a quitter, if that's what you mean."

He stepped toward her and Jacqui felt her heart pound in anticipation of his nearness.

"Sometimes it's better to quit while you're still ahead."

Her gaze drank in his face, the raw sexuality of his broad shoulders and lean hips. It was impossible not to imagine this man with women in his life. He was a man who had most everything a woman wanted.

"Meaning what?" she asked lowly.

The wry smile on his face changed to a regretful frown. "Meaning you should give up on me, Jacqui."

She stood motionless. "I can't do that."

He made an impatient sound and looked away from her. "You might as well," he said flatly. "This just isn't going to work. I was crazy to imagine it ever could."

"And what about last night?" she asked huskily, closing the gap between them. Her hands reached to cup his cheek as her body pressed into his. "Am I supposed to forget all about how it feels to touch you, to kiss you?"

Spencer swallowed as he gazed down at her. "Jacqui," he started, his voice full of torment, "why do you want to make it so hard?"

"You're the one making things hard," she argued. "When I want something, I'm not bashful about going after it. If I was, I wouldn't have become a jockey."

She leaned forward and brushed her lips against his. Spencer's hands reached out and clenched her waist. Her mouth was like sweet, warm honey. He couldn't resist the soft temptation. His mouth closed roughly over hers.

Jacqui felt both desire and frustration in his kiss, yet beneath all that she felt love. In that moment she knew that no matter what, she couldn't turn away or give up on him.

"I know what I want, Spencer," she said, once the kiss ended and her lips were nuzzling the warm skin of his neck. "I want you to put this fear of my riding behind you. So that we can be together—as man and wife."

Spencer pulled his head back just enough to enable him to see her face. At the moment he didn't know which was affecting him the most: the closeness of her body or her words.

"You're already married to the racetrack," he said in a low voice.

Her hands moved inside his jacket and slid up and down the front of his chest. His body reacted to her touch, even though he tried to keep the door shut on his heart. Spencer wanted to make love to her, to take possession of her soft little body until they were both so spent they couldn't argue.

"So are you, Spencer. But I love you. I'm willing to share you."

His brown eyes grew dark as his lashes slowly lowered until finally they hid his feelings from Jacqui.

"But I'm not willing to share you, Jacqui," he murmured. "Call me selfish, or call me a possessive man. I want a wife. Not a jockey for a wife."

"You want me. Right now," she countered huskily. "Just like I want you."

His eyelids lifted and Jacqui could see that he couldn't deny her words. She felt herself shudder with longing as his right hand lifted and cradled the back of her head. Jacqui rose on tiptoes to reach his lips and then everything else was a blur.

His mouth possessed hers, heatedly and hungrily and Jacqui felt a pulsing ache deep inside her that had her clutching him, urging her body closer to his.

"Spencer, I love you," she breathed as he began to unbutton her heavy coat. "Don't shut me out."

The garment fell open. With the barrier out of the way, Spencer's arms went around her, pulling her tightly against him. He could feel her breasts straining beneath the thin fabric of her blouse, and all he could think of was peeling away her clothes and letting her soft heat take away all the pain inside him.

Without stopping to think any further, Spencer lifted Jacqui off her feet and carried her until they reached the stacked hay bales.

Lying back against one of the lower wedges, he pulled Jacqui down with him. For long moments he kissed her, his hands meshed in her long, red hair, his tongue searching the intimate cavern of her mouth.

Jacqui was lost to the smell and feel of him, the freedom of touching him. Desire was overtaking her senses, blocking everything out but him. She pulled open the snap of his shirt and spread her hands across his bare chest. He groaned and shifted them both so that Jacqui was lying on the hay and he was above her.

"Jacqui," he whispered hoarsely, his hand seeking and finding her breast. "Do you know how much I want you? How much I've wanted you from the very first time I saw you?"

A small sob rose up in her throat. "It will always be like this between us. Whether you want it or not."

He looked at her through cloudy, half-closed eyes. "I want, Jacqui. I want this. You."

Her hips were cradling his and he moved sensuously against her in the age-old motion of lovemaking, Jacqui felt her eyelids fall, her fingers dig into his waist.

The next moment her blouse was pushed aside and his mouth was on her breast. Jacqui's senses splintered in all directions, and she knew if something didn't happen they were going to make love here and now, without protection or commitment on his part.

Spencer felt her stiffen ever so slightly, but it was enough to distract him, to allow cooling sanity to seep into his brain.

He couldn't make love to her like this, even though his body was screaming for him to. Levering himself away from her, he looked down at her flushed face.

It was incredible how much he loved her and wanted her. He hadn't known anything could be so deep, so all-consuming. And with the certainty of his love also came fear, because he had the suspicion that Jacqui was right. He could not change his feelings for her any more than she could change hers. So how was he going to live with it?

"I'm sorry, Jacqui."

"Sorry for what?"

He watched her lips form the words, and felt the urge to kiss her again. "Sorry because I can't accept things the way you want them."

Jacqui blinked. "You mean about the rides Friday?"

Sighing, he pulled away from her and began to fasten his shirt. "Yes, about the rides. It's just that I was hoping last night that you'd changed your mind. That you'd decided I did mean more to you than anything else."

Jacqui straightened her own clothing, then slid off the hay bales. Gently touching his arm, she said, "You do mean more to me than anything. But there has to be other things in our lives, too. You wouldn't be happy with just me, without your training."

Spencer's face twisted with anguish. "A part of me knows that's true, Jacqui. But the other part that lived with Danielle just isn't ready to believe it."

She reached for his hands and threaded her fingers through his. "I'm not trying to go against you, Spencer. I just need for you to accept all of me."

His face was solemn. "And part of you is being a jockey," he stated.

She nodded slowly. "Is that asking so much?"

"Right now it's asking a hell of a lot."

Jacqui let out a pent-up breath. "Well, I guess you're being honest with me, at least," she said, trying her best to keep her voice steady. Still there was a betraying tremble to her words.

"I never dreamed I'd fall in love again," he said with a smile on his face. "Much less with a jockey."

Jacqui forced herself to breathe deeply. Her hand was still on his arm and her body still craved being next to his. "I don't know why," she told him wryly. "You've worked around jockeys for years."

He suddenly grinned and Jacqui was relieved to see his mood lift.

"Yeah, but none of them fill out their riding silks in the places you do."

Jacqui laughed, her eyes twinkling. "So you've noticed the difference?"

He took her by the arm and began to lead her out of the barn. "I've noticed."

They reached the door and he released his hold on her to open it. Once they were outside in the cold night air, Jacqui turned to him.

"Are you still angry with me?"

"Most of the time I stay angry with you," he said, but the gentle touch of his hands on her face told her differently.

"Will you watch me ride Friday?"

Spencer couldn't believe her. Why did she ask and expect so much from him? "Do I look like a fool to you?"

"You look like the man I love," she said with certainty.

Frustrated, he lifted his face to the sky and felt the rain on his skin. "Don't push me, Jacqui. Just go back to the house and get out of this rain."

Jacqui decided it would be best to obey him. "Do I have hay in my hair?"

He looked at the mussed red waves framing her face and reached out to pick away the broken bits of straw.

Jacqui quickly raised her hand to stop him. "Don't do that. If I go back to the house without hay in my hair, Uncle Hadley will be disappointed in me."

Spencer uttered a curse under his breath. "I think I'll kick that old man's hind end."

Jacqui chuckled and raised up to kiss his cheek. "I'll tell him that for you," she said, turning away to leave.

Spencer watched her go with a host of mixed feelings going round and round in his head and his heart.

"Good night, Spencer," she called back to him.

He lifted his hand in acknowledgment, then watched her move on until the shadows of the stables swallowed up the sight of her.

Chapter Nine

Bob Barrett was an older man, short, with a thick mane of gray hair. Jacqui would have guessed him to be seventy at least and in some small way he reminded Jacqui of her dear Claude.

She liked him immediately once she met him at the racetrack. He gave her a quick rundown of both horses she'd be riding and any peculiarities she should know about.

Jacqui dressed for the fourth race with eager anticipation. The weather had turned warm and beautiful. The track was in perfect condition and there was a big crowd out to enjoy the horses and the spring weather.

For the past three days she and Spencer had kept up a truce of sorts. They'd had no more arguments, but then they'd both steered clear of talking racing, riding or loving.

Jacqui knew they were both just biding time. She'd decided to comply with his wishes and not push things. Yet she missed him terribly, even though they spent a great deal of time together. She needed his affection, his love, and she wondered how long they could skirt around the issue, how long they could be with each other without really being together.

Still she held on to the fact that he loved her. Jacqui had no doubts about his feelings for her. She could see it in his eyes when he looked at her. And she hoped that love would finally make him see there was no choice but for them to be married, to live out the rest of their lives together.

Hadley had come to the track with Jacqui today, but Spencer hadn't given her an answer as to whether he would show up.

As she joined Bob Barrett and her Thoroughbred mount Reelin' and Rockin' in the saddling paddock, she scanned the crowd, hopefully searching for his face. It shocked her when she saw him standing beside Hadley, his black hat pulled low over his forehead, a cigarette dangling from his mouth.

She gave the two men a tiny little wave, hoping the paddock judge wasn't watching her closely. Jockeys weren't allowed to communicate in any way with the crowd. But Jacqui couldn't help it this one time. She was happy to see Spencer even though he didn't look at all happy to be there.

Reelin' and Rockin' had drawn the number six gate. He was definitely tuned to run. When the gates popped open, he shot forward with a great lunge, and by the last turn he was well in the lead, pulling at least three lengths away from the rest. He sailed across the finish line, and Jacqui let out a long breath, standing up in the stirrups to tell her horse it was all over and he could coast now.

Bob Barrett was waiting for her. She pulled up her goggles and tossed him her bat after signaling to the stewards. Bob Barrett gave out a loud whoop as he led Jacqui and the horse into the winner's circle. Elated, Jacqui spotted Spencer and Hadley just outside the railing around the circle.

Hadley looked triumphant as he gave Jacqui a thumbs-up sign. Beside him, Spencer looked pale and resigned.

Jacqui's spirits sank. She didn't want to hurt him. She didn't want him to come to the track and watch her ride just to put him through an emotional wringer. She only wanted him to see that she was capable, that she wasn't in mortal danger every time she got astride a racehorse. But from the strained expression on his face, her victory wasn't having that kind of effect on him.

Jacqui finished a respectable third in her next race in spite of her horse stumbling at the starting gate. Mr. Barrett seemed fully satisfied and assured her she'd be hearing from him.

Once the races were over, Hadley drove back to the farm with Spencer, leaving Jacqui to follow on her own.

Throughout the drive, Jacqui's emotions swayed back and forth. There were two things she was certain of: she loved Spencer and she loved riding. The thing she wasn't sure about was how to blend them all together to show him things could work, that they could be happy.

By the time she arrived home, she'd decided the only choice she had left was to keep riding and to give Spencer more time to get used to the reality of her being a jockey. He'd come to see her today. At least that was a small start. Yet something in her heart told her the road ahead of her was going to be slow and difficult.

A week later Jacqui was in the jockey's quarters, dressing for her fifth and final race of the day.

The day had been hot, making the races even more grueling for the horses and the jockeys. For Jacqui's efforts so far, she had one victory, a third place, and two that had crossed the finish line out of the money.

It was not a day to be discontented with, however. Many jockeys went for days without a good race, much less a first or third. But as Jacqui pulled on her red silk shirt, she didn't feel the lift to her heart that she usually did when she prepared for a race.

No one had to tell her the reason for the depressed condition of her heart. It was Spencer. Or the lack of Spencer, she added to her grim thoughts.

For the past week he'd been like an indifferent stranger, doing his best to avoid her as they both worked around the farm. Several times Jacqui had tried to approach him, to tell him how much she still loved him, but each time he'd found an excuse to turn away.

Now Jacqui was doing her best to plod on with her day-to-day life, telling herself she'd chosen the only course that was right for either of them. But so far that course, whether right or wrong, was proving to be very painful for Jacqui.

Jacqui's final race was a Thoroughbred race. She would be riding a horse trained by Palmer Kirkland, a big gray gelding with a long lean body, aptly named Silver Blade. As Jacqui mounted him in the saddling paddock, she had the feeling she was on a winner.

When Jacqui and Palmer came onto the track for the post parade, she noticed there was a big crowd gathered next to the fence and the winner's circle. But Jacqui's eyes went straight to Spencer. Wearing a gray hat and a blue-striped shirt, he was standing near the finish line. A program was rolled up in his right fist and a cigarette was in his other.

His eyes caught and held Jacqui's as she rode by, but he did not lift his hand or acknowledge her in any other way. The sight of him was not only painful to Jacqui, but it was also confusing. He seemed to be trying very hard to put her out of his life. She couldn't understand why he was still coming to the track to see her ride.

"I haven't had the chance to ask you how you like living in Oklahoma," Palmer spoke, breaking into Jacqui's dismal thoughts.

She looked across at him and hoped the smile on her face didn't look forced. "I like it very much. Much more than I thought possible."

The line of horses had passed the grandstands and were now heading back down the track toward the starting gate. The sun was shining brightly, heating her skin through the silk of her red shirt. Beneath her, Silver Blade's coat glistened like blue steel.

She patted the horse's neck while her mind kept seeing Spencer standing by the fence and the stark look on his face as he'd watched her ride by. Jacqui wondered if he realized how much he was always in her thoughts. Could he possibly know that even on the track, he was always in her heart?

"I couldn't help but notice that you still haven't jockeyed any of Spencer's horses," Palmer commented. "I figured by now Spencer would have you mounted on everything he puts on the track."

Jacqui felt as if someone was wringing the blood from her. Not wanting to explain anything to this man, she said the first thing that came to her mind. "Spencer is very choosy when it comes to his horses. I haven't proven myself in his eyes yet."

Palmer grimaced. "He must be a blind man if he can't see you're a good jockey."

Looking straight ahead, Jacqui pinned her eyes on the gates. Spencer was blind, she silently agreed, but not in the way Palmer meant. Spencer was blind to the fact that they should be together, sharing their lives now, instead of worrying about what might happen in the future. But Jacqui was beginning to doubt that there was anything that could ever make him see this. Silver Blade was ready to run. Once the gates popped, he jumped out in the lead. Knowing he liked to run in the front, Jacqui let the big gray set the pace for the whole pack.

It wasn't until the third turn that the two horses behind her threatened to make a move on her lead. Knowing every inch she saved might make the difference in winning, Jacqui held Silver Blade as close to the rail as possible.

When the horses turned the last curve and started down the homestretch, the green of number five's colors flashed in the corner of Jacqui's eye as he came up on her right. Then suddenly, without warning, number five veered to the left, bumping into Silver Blade's hindquarters. It knocked Jacqui and her horse into the rail.

Spencer stood white-faced, his hands gripping the fence as he watched the gray horse reel under the impact of the collision.

"Jump, Jacqui!" he yelled, knowing there was nothing he could do to get to her, to help her.

"She's going to fall and be trampled!" someone yelled beside him, echoing his fears.

His heart in his throat, he watched the horse go down completely to its knees, throwing Jacqui upon its neck. Her batting quirt went flying through the air as she desperately grabbed the horse to keep from falling.

A split second of agony passed as Jacqui fought to hold on. Then to Spencer's utter amazement the horse gathered itself back together, and Jacqui was struggling to recover her seat in the saddle. There was no chance that Jacqui could ever regain the lead, but she seemed determined to take the gray across the finish line.

It was the most valiant, fearless effort Spencer had ever seen from a jockey. Tears blurred his eyes as he watched her and the horse fly across the finish. Not as a posted winner, but a winner just the same.

When Jacqui eventually made it back to the jockey's quarters, she went straight to the shower and stood for long minutes under a spray of cool water.

She was heartsick about the race. Not because she'd acquired a black bruise from her hip to her knee, or because she'd lost, but because the race meant there was virtually no chance of Spencer ever changing his mind about her riding now. Her near accident had surely clamped the door shut on his mind and his heart.

Jacqui suddenly knew she had but one choice left. She would give up racing. Spencer—and her love for him—came first in her life. He was the most important thing to her, even more important than riding. Losing her horses was something Jacqui could get over. But she could never get over losing Spencer.

Another woman jockey had been riding in the same race. She was dressing as Jacqui came out of the shower.

"That was tough luck, Jacqui," she said. "You had the race won."

Jacqui shrugged as she toweled moisture from her long hair. "It was just one of those unfortunate things."

Immediately after the race Jacqui had filed an objection with the stewards against the number five horse. After reviewing the video of the race, they had disqualified the horse, but that was only a small compensation to Jacqui.

Since there were still three races left for the day when Jacqui left the building and walked across the parking area, she had the place all to herself. It would be a relief not to have to fight the traffic leaving the grounds. Her leg was throbbing, and each time she thought of Spencer and the race, she wanted to burst into tears.

Her car was parked at the end of a row, next to a white van. She was searching in her handbag for her keys, and it wasn't until she lifted her head that she

saw Spencer standing beside her little car. The sight of
him startled her and she gasped softly.

"I didn't mean to frighten you," he said.

He was the last person she'd been expecting to see
and she stared at him for long moments. "I wasn't
expecting to see you here," she told him.

She stepped forward and unlocked the car. Spencer
felt his heart pound in his chest as his eyes traveled
over her. She was so soft and delicate, so full of courage and determination. She'd changed his life and she
was more precious to him than anything.

"I know we haven't done a lot of talking this past
week," he began, "but I—"

Jacqui looked up at him. As her eyes swept over the
handsome lines and angles of his face, she felt so
swamped with love that she was suddenly choked with
it.

"But what?" she went on for him. "You want to
bring home the fact that I could have been killed? You
want to tell me that when Silver Blade fell out there on
the track, that it justified everything you've been saying to me about my racing, about us?"

Before Jacqui knew what was happening, he
reached out and gathered her in his arms.

Dazed, Jacqui was suddenly aware that her cheek
was pressed against his shirt and his hands were on her
back, clutching her close against him.

"Oh God, Jacqui, when I saw your horse go down,
I felt—I'd never been more afraid. But then as I
watched you struggle to stay aboard—" He stopped
and shook his head. His hand came up and closed
around her thick damp braid. "Something else came
over me, Jacqui. I could suddenly see just how much

riding meant to you. You stayed on and fought to finish the race when most jockeys would have pulled up or bailed off. You really do love it, don't you?"

Tears were stinging her eyes, making her throat tight. She reached up and did her best to wipe her eyes with her fingertips. "Almost as much as I love you," she murmured shakily.

Spencer closed his eyes and pressed his cheek against her hair as he savored the feel of having her in his arms again.

"I'm so sorry, Jacqui. I know the words are late in coming. But it wasn't until I saw you out there today that I actually realized how selfish it was of me to ask you to give up your riding."

Jacqui's breathing stopped. She flattened her hands against his chest and pushed far enough away from him to see his face. "Spencer, what are you saying? Are you trying to tell me—"

There was a faint smile on his face when his hands reached to cup her cheeks. "I'm saying when Silver Blade fell it scared the hell out of me. But it also opened my eyes. When you slammed into the rail I'd be lying if I said I wasn't afraid for you, but when you held on and crossed the finish line, I was also very proud of you, Jacqui."

"Proud?" she echoed in stunned disbelief.

"Yes, proud. Proud of your courage, your determination. Proud of the woman you are." Groaning, he pulled her back against him. "I've been so single-minded, so caught up with my fears from the past that I couldn't see what I was doing to you, to us. Can you forgive me, Jacqui?"

Jacqui suddenly felt weak with happiness. She clung to his shoulders, needing and loving the solid strength he gave her. "Oh, Spencer, after Silver Blade went to his knees all I could think of was you—and that racing wasn't worth ruining the chance for us to be together."

Spencer crushed her a little tighter in his arms, "I think my heart knew it could never really give you up."

Jacqui looked up at him. "You've been coming to the track every day to watch me ride. I couldn't understand why."

His smile was wry as he looked into her eyes. Their green color shimmered with unshed tears and stabbed Spencer with the love he saw there.

"Why do you think? I love you, Jacqui. That could never change. And I couldn't stand thinking of you over here at the track, racing without me watching. In spite of everything, I wanted to be here in case you needed me."

The ache that had been in Jacqui's heart for so long disappeared. In its place was a happiness so sublime that she wanted to shout to the heavens.

"Before the race, when Palmer and I were riding to the gates, he made the remark that you were blind where I was concerned."

"Oh, he did," Spencer said, but there was no jealousy in his voice. Without a doubt he knew Jacqui's heart belonged to him. "Did he mean blinded to the woman, or the jockey?"

"The jockey," she answered. "He can't figure out why I'm not riding your horses."

Spencer suddenly shook his head and laughed. It was a true laugh, coming deep from within him. Jacqui had never heard a more beautiful sound.

"Well, it looks like Palmer is in for another surprise," he said, nudging the brim of his hat back on his forehead and giving her a beguiling grin.

"What do you mean?" she asked, not quite following his words.

His hands softly kneaded her shoulders. "I think we've already wasted too much time, don't you? You've been telling me what a wonderful pair we would make. Husband and wife. Trainer and jockey. Will you marry me on those terms, my darling, Jacqui?"

Her heart was so full, so content, that for long moments she merely looked up at him smiling, then finally she raised on tiptoes to touch her mouth to his. "I love you, Spencer. Love you so much."

Epilogue

Oklahoma was usually beautiful in late November, and on this particular day it was nothing but gorgeous sunshine.

It was the final race day at Blue Ribbon Downs for the season, and the stands were filled with people. Not only were they there to enjoy the horses and the wagering for the last time of the year, they were also there to see one of the season's biggest and most prestigious races—the Black Gold Futurity.

Bold Tyrant had qualified in the trials with the second fastest time in a field of ten horses.

Spencer was beside himself with pride. For the final race, he'd had special silks designed for Jacqui. White with black chevrons on the sleeves. She'd fastened a tiny white rose into her French braid. And not to let Bold Tyrant be outdone, she and Spencer had braided the horse's mane and the top portion of his tail and tied it with a black silk rose. He looked magnificent and Jacqui kissed the horse's nose before Spencer ponied them onto the track for the post parade.

"Now don't be nervous, sweetheart," Spencer told her as they passed in front of the grandstand. "Just give Tyrant the rein and he'll do it all for you."

Jacqui smiled to herself. Spencer always gave her bits of advice before each race. Jacqui loved him for it, even if she didn't always take it.

"Tyrant and I understand each other completely. He's all ready, aren't you boy?" she crooned to the horse.

Spencer looked at her and the horse and smiled. They made a beautiful sight, one that he'd been waiting to see for a long time. It was the last day, the big race, the big money, and the big honor. He wanted it all for Jacqui. These past months since they'd married had been the happiest in his life, and everything Spencer did he did for her.

Bold Tyrant was a nervous horse in the gates, but Spencer managed to hold his head straight on. When the gates opened, Jacqui got a clean break.

From that moment it was Bold Tyrant the whole four hundred and forty yards. In less than twenty-two seconds it was all over. Jacqui had won it by the margin of a nose.

It was chaos in the winner's circle. TV cameras and people surged around with congratulations as Spencer was presented with a trophy and Jacqui with a bouquet of roses.

Bold Tyrant was on a high from the run, and Spencer was doing his best to hold him steady among the commotion. Above it all, Jacqui looked down from her seat on the horse and caught Spencer's gaze. The pride and love on her face told him all he needed to know.

That night at the farm, Jacqui hurried to the bedroom to finish dressing. She wanted to be ready and waiting when Spencer returned from feeding down at the barn.

In the kitchen, the table was set with fine china, champagne was chilling, and candles waited to be lighted. Tonight was going to be a celebration for them both, one that she'd saved as a surprise for Spencer.

"Jacqui? Where are you, darling?"

"In here," she called him. "In the bedroom."

He appeared in the doorway, then stopped in his tracks when he saw her. She was wearing a deep purple dress that clung to her figure, and her hair, which had grown even longer since they'd married, hung loose around her shoulders like a shiny red cape. She looked up at him as she finished clipping amber-colored stones in her ears.

"My goodness, you look gorgeous," he said slowly while coming into the room. "Should I know what you're dressing up for?"

Smiling sassily, she rose from the dressing bench. "No. I've planned a celebration for us."

Spencer went to her and slid his arms around her waist. Jacqui raised on tiptoe, pulled his Stetson off, and kissed him thoroughly.

"I thought we'd finished celebrating Tyrant's win earlier this evening with Hadley," he said huskily.

She gave him a sly look. "Not quite. I thought we'd celebrate his victory a little more. And then I thought we'd celebrate our having a baby."

For a moment he looked stunned. "Jacqui! Are you pregnant?"

Her cheeks dimpled. "No. But starting tonight I hope to be."

His expression grew serious. "Jacqui, are you sure? Your riding will—"

She placed her finger against his lips. "I've had a wonderful year of racing. Now I want to give you a child. After it's a few months old I can always go back to riding. Gertrude is just dying to be a nanny. And I hope you're just dying to be a daddy," she added.

Without a word, he picked her up in his arms and tossed her on the bed.

"Spencer! What are you doing? Supper is waiting."

His fingers began to unfasten the buttons at her throat. "We can have supper at midnight," he murmured. "Right now I want to make love to the woman I adore."

Jacqui smiled and opened her arms to him. She was ready for the celebration to begin.

*   *   *   *   *

At long last, the books you've been waiting for by one of America's top romance authors!

DIANA PALMER

DUETS

Ten years ago Diana Palmer published her very first romances. Powerful and dramatic, these gripping tales of love are everything you have come to expect from Diana Palmer.

In March, some of these titles will be available again in **DIANA PALMER DUETS**—a special three-book collection. Each book will have two wonderful stories plus an introduction by the author. You won't want to miss them!

Book 1
SWEET ENEMY
LOVE ON TRIAL

Book 2
STORM OVER THE LAKE
TO LOVE AND CHERISH

Book 3
IF WINTER COMES
NOW AND FOREVER

Silhouette Books®

DP-1